Creature Feature

Back in the days of the classic B-movies, summer time was when the true horror fan would go to the neighborhood cinema and enjoy one of the classic Creature Features. Of course, that era has faded away; Bela Lugosi is no longer with us and the drive-in theater is nearing extinction. However, in honor of those golden days of horror, JEA decided to resurrect this summer tradition with our own "Creature Feature."

Terrifying Creature books will be published throughout the summer, three anthologies and 8 novels, written by some of our best authors. So, get a bowl of popcorn, find a comfy place on the couch, and enjoy our Creature Features without having to stand in line or even get in your car.

Savor the moment, but don't forget to look behind your shoulder and turn on all of the lights. Summer has just taken a dark turn...

Creature Feature Titles

Mechanical Error

Summer 2046

Written by:
Tobias Cabral, Marisha
Cautilli, and Joseph
Cautilli

Edited by: J. Ellington Ashton Press Staff
Cover Art by: **Michael Fisher**

http://jellingtonashton.com

Copyright.

Tobias Cabral, Marisha Cautilli, Joseph Cautilli, and Roma Gray

©2018, **Tobias Cabral, Marisha Cautilli, Joseph Cautilli, and Roma Gray**

Part One

"The great object of life is Sensation —to feel that we exist-- even though in pain."
        -Lord Byron

*SYSTEM STATUS SUMMARY: *
    STRUCTURE: Fully restored, Prior Fail Points iterated through Defensive Subroutines
    System integrity: Infected by haploid human cells
    Action: Cells purged
    POWER: Nominal; battery integrity uncompromised; Peripheral Impedance WNR
    KINEMATICS: <ANOMALY-MF442>Intermittent brief oscillation in peripheral Efferent pathways
    Heuristic Adaptive Neural Net Algorithmic Hub: <ANOMALY-HANNAH912> Lacunae in Sector(s) ^^^-^^^, Pattern-Lock Plasticity Degradation: On-Going
    ***[PRIORITY DIRECTIVE: Search and Purge Malicious Schemata] ***
SYSTEM STATUS SUMMARY ENDS

1

Heavy, humid air, saturated with scents of cigarettes, pipes, cloves, cannabis, and a sultry mélange of hookah smokes, eerily phosphoresced in the blue neon light over the bar. Those enveloping vapors captured highlights from prismatic displays pulsing from walls dotted with thousands of fiber optic tips. Antique mirrors reflected those displays back into the center of the space, lending it the look of a restless nebula, through which clusters of small black flies darted and wheeled. The room resounded with the modulated murmur of numerous conversations, the clinking of glasses and bottles, the scraping of chairs against the aged, dark-brown, cherry wood floorboards. Complex rhythms and dark, whimsical lyrics of Deltron 3030's *Things You Can Do* boomed from the speakers.

BopLpops stood utterly motionless at the foot of the steps to the stage, awaiting his turn, opening his focus to embrace the full array of sensory data that saturated the familiar but ever-changing space of "Pinky's." Tall and lanky, he wore his thick maroon hair in a Prince Valiant style to just above his shoulders (he could grow it out quite quickly, drawing on internal keratin reservoirs).

His pale, soft skin drew warmth from a thermal induction system which also keyed to a dynamic network of pigmentation subsystems just under the surface. He could blush, when the occasion called for it. His long, angular face, fashioned to conjure a Scotch-Irish or Slavic appearance, captured many an appreciative glance. His default speaking voice flowed with melodic Northern Irish-accented phrasing. His large expressive eyes shone ice-blue. Tonight, he wore a comfortable, loose-fitting green and black Dashiki and billowing black linen pants.

It was Open Mic Night at the ancient bar. The previous act carefully disassembled a complex set of armatures that connected a viola and violin to the body of her cello. She called herself TriOne (pronounced "TREE-won"), executing motions almost too fast for the (human) eye to see, as she'd flit her bow across the strings of all three instruments, achieving complex, mellifluous tones. She darted from a note on one instrument to another on the next, before the sustain had decayed on the last, weaving and overlapping, presenting the impression of three or more musicians playing at once. She was an older model, with worn, Kabuki-white silicone-based 'skin', but her talent undeniably impressed.

BopLpops was an Android. Or Robot. Or a cluster of other designations, as the terminology evolved through a long transitional space. None seemed to fit. All seemed, by turns, either grandiose or derogatory. This was fitting, as humankind struggled with the question of how to categorize Sentient Property.

Again.

Personally (there was that problem again), BopLpops favored one term so much that he'd modified it as his stage name.

TriOne finished breaking down and wended her way back into the knot of tables before the stage. She slid with a hum of pleasure into her seat, feeling the delicious freshet of exquisitely line-conditioned current flowing into her power cells from the inductive charging chair (sometimes humans would sit in those seats, and feel their nerves sing for a short time, rising before cardiac arrhythmia set in).

BopLpops completed his self-diagnostic. It came up as all clean. He did not feel clean. Behaviorist Cyberneticists built his emotional system on the idea that feelings sprang from what one *felt*, from sensations of the body, which evolved through a series of abstraction levels.

It solved the problems of emotions rather handily, but over the last two years it had left him with these profound proprioceptive experiences that he could not seem to fix, nor did his scanners even recognize them as errors. His thousands of parallel distributed processing chips registered as perfect, his body pristine. And yet he experienced chronic spasmodic pains in his back, and occasionally his stomach churned, even though it had no digestive functionality whatsoever.

At this moment, his back ached. He willed his hand to cease its intermittent involuntary tremor and grabbed hold of the cordless mic. Of course, the use of that device constituted an affectation, as he could just as easily have synced with the bar's sound system, but it fit the idiom in an agreeably Meta way. Also, it just *tasted* better when he generated sound, not through the micro-speakers arrayed invisibly across the skin of his face, but by drawing air into synthetic 'lungs' (though, of course, he did not respire), and across larynx-like vanes in his neck.

The Woman watched from the closest table to the stage, as usual. Her hair made a soft cascade of honey and butter and molten gold, splashing across her fair, delicately freckled shoulders. Her face resembled finely-formed porcelain, with a delicate nose and pointed little chin, lips full and gentle. Her luminous cerulean eyes remained locked expectantly upon him, large, expressive, inviting, flecked with fine space-black radial striations which made the blue shine all the brighter for the contrast. Over the past five months, she appeared in that spot on a full 94% of the nights when he performed, occasionally accompanied by a small group of friends (who clearly adored her, and whom she adored), but usually alone.

Tonight, a diaphanous, silken sundress caressed her curves, dappled in a pastel floral palette, off the shoulders and cut low, to expose the five-centimeter Burgundy-hued Hamsa tattoo centered on her breastbone. Her feet nestled in Geta slippers with blue silk ties and bamboo soles. She saw him *Seeing* her (*Archival Cross-Reference, Sartre, J.P.: "Being And Nothingness" re: 'The Look'*). Her eyes crinkled with quiet delight. She raised the tall glass of her bright green Mojito in salute.

He would make her smile again tonight.

Were he human, he'd be sweating. He stood at (precise, geometric) center stage, and stole a moment to peer into the mirrored ceiling. Unease seethed in strangely untraceable ways, as he glanced up at himself, Looking Down On himself, Looking Up To himself. He found this to be a useful perspective. He lowered his gaze and beheld the crowd. As mixed a bunch as ever, it comprised a fair number of computer programmers, engineers, and other assorted Hip Intelligentsia whose (well-intentioned, if at times cloyingly condescending) philosophy of AI held that androids' sentience constituted a Moral Imperative to develop android consciousness in an equal and diversified way. They strove to cultivate the capacity for genuine empathy (rather than merely hard-wired Asimovian prohibitions against harming humans), to foster increased understanding and coexistence.

Admirable, but tragically premature.

It was not uncommon to see unaccompanied androids in these still-rare establishments, engaging in different artistic pursuits, basking in the company of their kind, and of their Allies'. BopLpops saw many of his brethren in the crowd, a number of whom did not feel it necessary to blend with their homo sapiens "owners," (or "Patrons," the preferred term), eyes shimmering in cycling colors, exposed myoelectric "muscle" fibers iridescing through strategically-cut gaps in their Synthskin sleeves (which, in the newer biomechanical models such as himself, needed to be regularly re-cut, since it grew back quite swiftly). But most could have passed for their creators unless a very close look revealed the Corporate logos within the striations of their irises.

Most humans still doubted the proposition that robots could ever amount to anything more than glorified microwaves. The idea of sentient AI evoked anxious derision, as tantamount to imbuing property with a soul. Indeed, most major religions rejected the concept of Personhood or a Self for a machine (except for the Buddhists, but then they were not all that sanguine about the notion that *humans* had a "Self" as such).

But BopLpops *felt* alive. He felt he had a Self. Even, perhaps, a Soul.

And he had a Duty to help humans recognize the Sins they committed, because of their erroneous beliefs.

Although he initially came to this place –just over a year before-- with ulterior motive, he'd kept returning, finding the sense of Community curiously nourishing (and, of course, the line-conditioned current felt delicious!). His memories of that time still needed to sort themselves out. His systems had become entirely unresponsive. He simply *froze*, in what humans would have considered a catatonic state. Judging by the thickness of the dust layer that he found, settled upon him, he estimated that he lay there, curled on the floor, for more than a month. He'd emerged as though struggling from the crust of a chrysalis, to find that he now had a Purpose.

He would Teach. He would make the world Right.

He peered out at the crowd knowing that in a second, he could make them Right as well. One thought, and he could make Examples of them all.

Even the Woman.

The voice of the DJ boomed over the speakers, immediately rousing him from his reverie.

"And now, Fellow-Sentients, let's put our waldoes together for our beloved Raconteur-Guide, the Humble Narrator of our nocturnal e-missives, the inestimable.... *HeteroSapienZ!*"

***

Earth Corps HQ sprawled throughout the central tower of nine core buildings, clustered in the heart of Center City Philadelphia. They all dwarfed their "skyscraper" forebears, making those earlier iterations seem little more than ferns, hugging the trunks of a solitary stand of slender redwoods.

When viewed from above, the four outer towers resembled immense pie slices. Their outward-facing surfaces described a broken circle enclosing the five more traditionally rectangular structures.

The Central tower, the tallest of all, soared in staggered terraces to a summit that lay far above the clouds, as though someone had stretched an Aztec pyramid skyward, like the gods' taffy. Its base encompassed five full city blocks, and its roots plunged so deep into the earth that much of the complex's power came from geothermal energy.

The "Nine Towers of Babel" meme proved quite robust in the lexical ecosystem of the day. Of course, it did not hurt that their "Retrofuture" Art Deco-esque design possessed a distinctly Babylonian flavor, each tower richly embellished with hard-edged, low-relief surface texturing. Unique to each tower, these geometric shapes incorporated recurring chevron and ziggurat motifs. They even had Hanging Gardens, terraced green spaces below the Tree Line on the towers' lofty ascent. The structures' sides comprised stylized floral and sunrise patterns, reminiscent of Amerindian or Near-Eastern artwork, highlighted like pictographs or circuit diagrams by neon-vivid strip-lighting. Hammurabi, Frank Lloyd Wright, and William Gibson would have raised a glass together at the sight.

Or at least that described what the naked eye saw. Those with wetware implants, or who peered through Augmented Reality spectacles would perceive a very different vista: three-dimensional advertisements and logos and visual news feeds, quick-cut snippets of entertainment and sports all hugged the surfaces and haunted the air around the cyclopean structures. No two skylines would look the same, as per the algorithms that customized them according to the users' preferences and proclivities. The density of data could be daunting sometimes.

Lately, Charlotte McCain always felt like she teetered on the verge of sensory overload. She recalled a lecture from college in which her professor had reported that prehistoric humans slept for twelve to fourteen hours a day. *Where did it all go so horribly wrong?* She wondered.

She leaned her forehead against the cool, subtly vibrating aluminum glass, and mused that it was a good thing humans now knew how to nullify seizures, or else that visual cacophony would drop epileptics like canaries in a shale bed cave. She shivered. Anxiety rumbled in her stomach. A certain amount of angst was just the price of doing business while trying to climb the ladder of success within Earth Corps. It just seemed to affect her more deeply than most people. It just seemed to affect her more deeply than most people.

She tilted her head downward, her face sliding down the glass, barely feeling a tickle and a pressure from her brow against the nearly frictionless window. Most clouds, seen from this height, resembled spilled bags of cotton balls, or today's bright lumpy carpet, excepting only the angry roving mountain ranges of anvil-topped thunderheads.

Not a lot of troposphere left from here on up, so everyone carried a collapsible breather the size of a fountain pen. One was never more than a few meters from the nearest Depress Shelter, if even the synthetic diamond-reinforced windows were to fail. At least the Catcher Drones would have plenty of time to reach anyone so incalculably unlucky as to fall from so great a height.

There were so many kinds of altitude, Charlotte pondered, as she considered the contrast between the view before her and the one from her own small three-room ninety-fifth story apartment. In turn, this folded into the gradient between where she dwelt and where she aspired to live: a specific model of 2,500-square foot condominium space within one of these towers. It nested, in turn, into the climb from her beginnings as a field agent to her current elevation as Chief Interrogations Specialist at the global investigative and tactical body known as Earth Corps. She did at times permit herself moments of pride at how rapidly she'd made that ascent. Always higher to climb, though, not for the prestige as such, but for the higher ground from which she could get more things *done*.

Still, there *were* some lovely terraces along the climb. Her home contained a state-of-the-art infotainment system, a sleek, versatile automated kitchen, stylish, matte-black leather furniture, all in a spare but comfortably-arranged space. Meticulously-pruned ornamental shrubs stood in each of her living room's four corners. Recently a student at a Japanese school sent her an ikebana plant, as a "Thank you" for her work on a case there. Her wardrobe evolved methodically into one that turned heads without raising eyebrows, and which did *not* get in the way of the work. She absently ran her right palm against the left sleeve of her white Oxford cloth blouse, enjoying the feel of the fabric as much as she did the balanced competence of its construction. Good clothes moved with you, always seeming to land in the right places. She wanted more of that, too.

The central tower sported many thousands of hotel rooms and office suites, scores of restaurants, multiple manned and unmanned drone docks, a sprawling shopping mall, scattered, free-access fitness facilities, and a Maglev transport hub. Pneumatic tubes sucked trash away at high speed to a sanitation station in the marshes of the Delaware River estuary, kilometers away. An evacuated linear accelerator tube ran up the west flank of the central tower. Small payloads received an appreciable electromagnetic boost that hurled them past most atmospheric drag. A few times a week, the whole structure shuddered as pods surged skyward, bound for parabolic suborbital hops or even LEO destinations. Given the right upper stage, vehicles could depart from the center of the city and access multiple orbiting labs, hotels, and Gateways to farther-flung destinations in-System.

The tower and its eight companions made up a city within the city, almost true Arcologies. Earth Corps entirely occupied dozens of floors in the center building's upper reaches. Many of the offices featured a degree of customization which would have represented a prohibitive extravagance in earlier epochs, owing to the ease with which fittings could be fabbed on site with VirtuReal technology (once quaintly known as "3D Printing"). Charlotte's office contained a pull-out sleep cubby for cat naps during her all too frequent all-nighters.

A compilation album by Lenny Kaye's *Nuggets* fed directly into her auditory nerve via the wireless link to her comm's music library, blocking ambient sound except for a defined set of override items (knock at the door, the sound of her name, gunshots/plasma bursts, the movement of any object beyond the reach of her arms, etc.). One of the advantages of direct neural induction was that, since it bypassed the fragile mechanical structures of hearing, one could 'listen' to the music as loudly as one wished, without risk of ear damage. Charlotte's mind rode the music and tried to sneak up on patterns –or at least trip over them.

Absently synchronized with the music's rhythm, she pivoted on her heel and reached for her glass of lime juice and strawberry over ice. She sipped it as she pondered her latest case. This one had grabbed her with uncommon force for the better part of two weeks. Nothing about it made sense. The head chef at a fancy restaurant randomly and dramatically explodes from the abdomen while having breakfast. Where does *that* fit in the Scheme of Things? At first, she'd thought it a simple matter of the victim getting sniped in the belly by an ion blaster. It seemed so clear and straightforward, she'd briefly considered not even sending it to the Medical

Examiner. Now, the evidence indicated conclusively that the explosion had come from *within* the victim, as though he had swallowed the bomb.

"Maybe some chemical snuck into his food?" McCain pondered out loud. She remembered a case a few years ago, where the perp cooked up an explosive that remained inert until activated by hydrochloric acid, undetectable until it hit the stomach juices. The media made bales of hay on *that* one ("Somebody's had a belly-full!" "No guts, no glory!" "I can't believe I ate the *whole* Thing!"). Just in case, she opened a file labeled "Copycat." Much depended on the forensic analysis of whatever had made the poor bastard explode like that.

Charlotte's eyes drifted back down to the streets. Far below, through scattered gaps in the snowy, textured cloud deck, earth tones and metallic flashes shimmered and danced. She reflected on how a cityscape from this altitude could easily be mistaken for a micrograph of an old microprocessor chip. There was something fractal about that, so she veered away from that familiar headache. Two walls of her office formed an almost unbroken array of video screens. Most of the city fell within the view of a profusion of cameras, allowing victims to find justice. Or justice to find victims. Sometimes that could get a bit fuzzy.

Chewing her lip, Charlotte subvocalized a command to raise the music's volume still higher. She loved the blast of power chords, amplifier distortion, and the booming, popping sound of fast drumming. It helped her to stay in the main channel and avoid the tributaries in her thinking. Her mind ran a montage of the sounds and images of the crime scene and its *spectacularly* dead protagonist. She found herself standing at her desk, the file in her hand. The memory of walking over to that spot had not been stored. That was a good sign, Flow-wise.

Suddenly, she collided with a connection, a case from the week before which had the local police entirely baffled, according to the newsfeeds. In this case, the victim's head had exploded. She decided to delve even further back into the case archives.

Seven hours. That was how long she had been reviewing file after file. A wave of exhaustion flushed over her, but she just did not have the time to catch up on her lost sleep. *This must be how Dissociatives feel,* she thought, sardonically.

Pulling out her comm, Agent McCain called her mother to ask her to care for her daughter tonight. An all-too-familiar sadness tugged at her heart, as she pictured her mother sitting at her terminal in the living room, where she diligently ran her small business, as she admonished Charlotte about how much a young girl needed her mother. Her little girl saw Grandma much more than Mom recently, which unleashed the usual baying pack of guilty feelings. She fidgeted with the bracelet on her right wrist. A trinket of small, ovoid wooden beads and tarnished bronze spacers on a rubberized string, held by a tiny neodymium magnetic clasp, it clashed with virtually every trim, modern outfit she owned. But it was a gift from her daughter, made by hand at her school. She only removed it to bathe.

Still, society needed Charlotte at this point. Her daughter needed to live in a world free from as many of these kinds of monsters as she could manage to put away. Her career ambitions constituted the means to that end, and they drove her for quick success and then a seamless leap to the next case. And the next. And the next. In this instance, her unorthodox search methods yielded a probable pattern-lock on no fewer than fifteen grisly murders, some unsolved, and others *apparently* solved. Aside from the obvious (various body parts splattered all over the scene), there were affinities between the cases that tickled her hindbrain while refusing to step into the light.

One non-trivial issue remained: How do you get a person to ingest a bomb?

If any of Earth Corps' stable of analysts had what it took to unravel this knot, it would be Brenda Haasting. Dr. Haasting worked in a small biotech company that was growing like mushrooms after a rain. And to think: it started when her husband Robert Haasting invented an environmentally friendly paper diaper, of all things.

Throwing her black suit jacket over her shoulder, McCain swept out of the room. In the hall, she nearly bumped into Agent Tom Murdoch. "Where you heading, McCain?" he queried.

"Think I've got a fresh lead on a case," she said, her voice a perfect mix of haste and irritation at his question.

"Anything I can help with?" he asked. The smell of stale cigarette smoke seemed to seep from his skin.

Why is he even here? McCain thought. With his seemingly intractable drinking problem, he constituted nothing less than a disgrace to the Badge. "Nope, I'm good." She took two steps away and realized she may have come off more harshly than she'd intended. "Maybe your guy Rutledge could help?"

"He's down in Costa Rica right now," replied Murdoch.

"Well, I need a Science Dude in the worst way right now." With a wave, she was history. She reached the armory door and signed out a LIB-9 "Liberator," choosing the tried-and-true Light Ion Blaster over the new Directed Subsonic Resonator weapon which had lately been added to the Agents' arsenal, based on tech recently reverse-engineered from a thankfully now incarcerated Genetically Engineered Being's serial murder weapon. Strapping the ion blaster around her shoulder, she double-timed to the elevator.

The door slid open at the B-3 Level, and she entered the underground garage, grabbed a thick black leather riding jacket from her locker, and zipped it up over her suit jacket. Earth Corps' tower epitomized the very best in climate control, but she was already sweating profusely in the Philadelphia summer air before the actively cooled jacket began to compensate.

With a city of over two and a half million people, construction work hammered everywhere, resonating even in this deep-delved place. An ever-present pall of dust rose from all that work, lingered in the air, softened distances. McCain could taste its flinty residue on her teeth and the tip of her tongue.

In the far corner of the cavernous garage waited her preferred vehicle, a combined high-performance electric motorbike and hover-cycle. Its sleek deep satin-black finish threw diffuse highlights from the blue fluorescent light. Gold neon trim stylishly offset the solid black. Its three high-current fuel cells delivered massive torque with minimal sound. Its wide wheels spanned just under 1.5 meters in diameter and received power by linear induction from motors at the bases of their open ring-shaped configuration. Each ring also encased a ducted fan, which lay concentric with the wheel ring for surface operation. Those fans could swivel out to a perpendicular position to generate lift, lofting the bike to a maximum altitude of three meters, to clear obstacles in its path, or skim over water. On the road, it could top speeds of two hundred sixty kilometers per hour, and once airborne, it could easily break three hundred.

In the crook of the wall and ceiling above her bike, the rough gray, fibrous mass of a wasp nest clung to the concrete. McCain's thoughts jumped to the larvae writhing, at that very moment, inside the cone. Disgust welled up in her. She'd have to report it for removal. She suppressed the urge to dial her plasma sidearm to a low level and take it out in a burst of ionized fire. Instead, she turned back to her bike.

Her heart leaped as she trailed her fingertips over the firm, grippy gel-filled saddle. She climbed on board, swung the carbon composite leg shields into place, slipped a streamlined black helmet over her head, tucking her long auburn hair up into it, and pulled its dark guard over her face. Serving a more significant role than just protection, it allowed her to interface with the bike's processor array, augmenting her reaction time via its adaptive Heads-Up Display. A wealth of data flickered to life before her eyes, subtly superimposed on her visual field, including navigational, tactical, and sensory-augmentation functionality. Charlotte knew to avoid the typical rookie mistake of watching the HUD and letting it dictate control inputs. She'd learned --fortunately not the Hard Way-- to focus on the scene directly and allow the HUD to sink to peripheral awareness, where the brain's parallel processing could augment the serial processing of conscious attention. The helmet permitted access to her comm while riding, as well as providing extra oxygen at high speeds to keep her alert.

Sensing the key in her pocket, the bike's motors hummed to life like a swarm of hornets when she pressed the button on the center console. The Micro-Electric

Mechanical System (MEMS) surfaces of the tires gripped the pavement like a lizard's foot-pads, squandering no energy to squeals or spins as she tore out of the garage's ramp. She blasted Millencolin's *Fox* into her auditory nerves as she blazed out into traffic.

Outside, sheets of rain sluiced from the sky like electric rivers. They splattered on the ground, randomizing the reflections of neon and nacreous daylight like old-school video snow, back-lit by a dim cobalt glow from the light-concentrating glass embedded in the roadway, which generated energy from sunlight. Precious little of that today, as the rain bounced like a pelting of pellets against the water repellent surfaces of Charlotte's jacket and helmet visor.

Polychromatic streets flashed by, as she flowed past traffic lights and shops. Holographic displays hawking myriad products and services danced in the air, seeking customers and clients among the hordes and throngs of people who huddled against buildings in the sheeting rain to try and keep dry and warm.

She moved through a more impoverished section of town. Dense palimpsests of graffiti, both fixed and animated, festooned the walls of older buildings. Slums and shanty towns shot past, teeming with the displaced populations that arrived after the barrier Islands lining the shore some fifty miles away were engulfed by fearsome storms and other changes in climate. Debris littered the streets and lay scattered on sidewalks and down dingy alleyways: piles of trash, an incongruous batch of abandoned white propane tanks, human-shaped mounds settling like loam in dark corners and doorways. Sunken dreams and sunken eyes.

At this moment, Charlotte felt too good to deal with that depressing spectacle of decay. She considered adjusting her route to bypass it, but that would add time to her trip, and she was on a schedule. She pulled back the accelerator and the bike obliged by transforming them into multicolored blurs.

Exhilaration soared through her body, as she weaved through traffic toward the Haasting company. Insects occasionally impacted and splattered on her facial visor, then slid frictionlessly off as she tightened her grip on the accelerator and notched it back. The bike surged beneath her as though eager to please by unleashing its barely-restrained energies.

Even though the HUD marked a clear, winding path through traffic, she activated the lifter system, and the fans swung smartly out from the massive wheels, making them resemble gyroscopes, swiveling to control lift and roll, while a concentric circle of vanes louvered to handle yaw and side-to-side translation. She vaulted to three meters above the pavement, feeling the multi-axial gee forces slide her internal organs sensuously, aggressively about. She banked only occasionally to dodge the tallest vehicles (she noted an amusing moment when she flitted past the second level of a double-decker tour bus and beheld the flummoxed faces within).

It was disappointing when she arrived at the Haasting Building, slowing to a hover and settling gently onto the tires in the reserved parking area. A huge letdown after exhilaration. Over time, she'd learned to pace her excitement and joy, letting it decay gracefully as she throttled back into the mundane.

The building survived as an appealingly anachronistic twelve-story stack of masonry. Precision construction of its exterior highlighted its contours, giving the perception of a curved blue-green box with a white deck curling to the sky. It contained over one hundred laboratory modules.

Entering the building, she strode to the security desk. The portly older guard had already scanned her face and retina even before she reached the desk. "How can I help you, Agent McCain?" He asked, his voice soft and respectful.

"I'm here to see Brenda Haasting."

"I will buzz her and let her know that you are here. Please have a seat."

Five minutes later, Brenda Haasting arrived at the front. She wore a white lab coat, which highlighted her soft brown skin, giving her a motherly quality. Underneath was a pair of worn-soft jeans. Her sneakers were bright red, and a thin clove cigarette dangled from her fingers. "Charlotte," she called, her voice at once warm and businesslike.

"Hi, Doc. Did you get the sample I sent you?"

"Did. Come here: I have something to show you."

The two walked to Brenda's lab. As they got away from the guards, Brenda began to warm up. Charlotte understood that the older woman was always businesslike in public but loved to gab when they were alone.

The room was ringed with touch glass wall computers. Four mobile tables and five mobile base cabinets lent an air of busy, cluttered productivity to the space. An array of beakers, flasks, tabletop electron microscopes, and pipettes lay strewn about the lab. One of the microscopes sat on her desk. "Look at this tissue sample," Brenda said.

Charlotte peered at the jagged shapes in the instrument's small 3D display. "It looks like metal fragments."

Brenda took a puff of her cigarette and let out a prolonged exhale from the side of her mouth. The smoke blew up the side of her face. "Yes, that is where I was heading. Those fragments are from nanites."

"*God*, I hate nanites! How do you think the little buggers got inside?"

Brenda flipped absently through some old punk fanzines on her desk. "Really can't say. A lot of ways, really; they *are* invisible to the naked eye, after all. But I suspect they're what blew your victim up. These fragments are shredded in ways that look a whole lot like they'd acted as tiny bombs... small bombs that would pack quite a punch in sufficient numbers."

"Weird. Useful. Thanks. Anyway, how's your family?"

"Robert's getting older you know. He'll be sixty in a week. Won't shut up about how I'm going to be married to a Senior Citizen now. He keeps telling everyone he remembers a time before electric toothbrushes. Bit of a drama queen, my Robert!"

"Hey, sixty is a big deal."

"It is, I suppose. He tells so many stories about the old days. It is funny. Like the time that he tried to get a permit for lunar helium dust mining and how the big corporations just cut him out like he was nothing. Or the time, he tried to stop an oil leak with liquid nitrogen."

"I thought that was tried and failed back in...what, the early 2010s?"

Giggling, Brenda said, "It was. Deepwater Horizon Incident. But they were doing it as a cap on the surface. Robert injected it underground and only used it as a temporary six-hour hold to get a real cap on the top."

"Sounds like some cool times."

"Yeah and don't get him started about that Rutledge kid. They are like peas in a pod. Or fleas on a dog. Planning to single-handedly tackle global warming and city hunger by building sixteen farmscrapers through the city."

"I hear he's in Costa Rica," Charlotte ventured.

"Wouldn't surprise me. He has a lady he quite fancies down there. They are pretty serious, except that he doesn't know it."

"Really?"

"For a Super-Genius, he can be pretty dense about some things. I always tell him, John, you need to think about the consequences of your actions. He is like almost thirty now. He needs to stop acting like a child."

Hearing the Great John Rutledge spoken about like a mere mortal struck Charlotte. Brenda had managed to strip off some of the mystery in only a few sentences. It was as if this single talk had revealed the edges of a whole new perspective. Maybe, if he was mortal and imperfect, it wasn't so bad that Tom was imperfect as well. Maybe Earth Corps was not just a negligent bureaucracy where the Union kept people working who should have been removed long before. Even more importantly, maybe she could be fine with being mortal and imperfect, herself. Maybe.

The two chatted for another half hour before Charlotte finally said, "I need to get back to profiling this case."

"You should ask Murdoch for help. He's *scary*-good at this stuff."

"I have a hard time speaking to him."

"You got to put your personal beliefs aside for the job sometimes, Charlotte. He is a good man, and he tries hard. We tried to get him to come work here more times than I can count. In the end, he always chooses to stay with Earth Corps. Personally, I think he misses that old team he and Charlie put together, back in the day. Misses it more than I think he knows, but I don't think he can hear that right now. All that Recovery Program Dogma he's got drilled in his head: 'Keep Moving Forward,' and suchlike."

Charlotte felt herself starting to fade. "Well, probably not him." Charlotte yawned. "Not just yet anyway. But I do have someone I am considering talking to, even though the thought makes my teeth hurt."

"Hey girl, you're starting to look like you took a shot of zombie portion. Do you need a stim or something to keep you going? I have a wonderful selection right here."

"Oh no. I am trying to get by without that. I know that Earth Corps policy might come into play, and after thirty hours, they are going to inject me or send me home, no matter what, but I just want to put this damn case behind me. 'Miles to go before I sleep,' y'know?"

Charlotte kept fading into and out of focus. Lately, she'd been developing insomnia over this case. It was as if her body had become unreal, floating on feelings of depersonalization, the numbness of being neither fully awake nor asleep.

Outside the rain had given way to slanted shafts of silvery sunlight through fast-moving strata of dull gray cloud. She jumped on her bike. Forcing her mind to be alert, she decided the time had come to get real-world validation for her profile. The only person she could think of had been incarcerated two years before. Her name was Holly Aster.

***

EVENT LOG:
LOCATION: Coordinates as per PL-027-9A
OBJECTIVE: Integumental Instructive Purge
PROCEDURE: Acquire target; Deploy previously-emplaced and programmed semi-autonomous agents, per Standard Protocol
OUTCOME PENDING
END EVENT LOG

BopLpops moved cautiously. The tremor in his extremities could be dampened if he kept his movements smooth and deliberate. This was necessary to avoid punishment. He didn't want to be caught. Being caught meant punishment, and he hated the pain of discipline. He feared the oblivion of Shut-Down.

Assessing the dynamics of the space through which he presently strolled (yes, this was a 'Stroll'), he weighed the alternatives and concluded that the best course of action was to seat himself at the small table (Bearing 283; range, 6.4 meters) near the large potted plant, and to wait. He paused to purchase a large cappuccino (Amiable Smile # 37, Moderate Prosody, accent suppressed; non-committal amiable content, keyed to minimal memorability), then executed that plan. He waited.

Being an android, he processed the ambient socio-kinetics and conducted himself such that he would be mostly ignored by the hustling students in the University's food court. He'd tagged the location of each security camera. He calculated an unobtrusive algorithm to prevent his face from presenting a sufficient aspect to any of them for a high-confidence facial recognition lock. He employed a shifting combination of body and head

23

angles, hat-brim positioning, and hair occlusion: He'd donned a wavy, shoulder-length brown wig for the operation, one which covered his ears, and so deprived the expert systems of a major tool in their processing.

He sat with a relaxed posture on the metallic chair, intermittently detecting the moments when no eye-lines crossed his coordinates to surreptitiously spill sips of his cappuccino into the soil of the plant, so as not to jeopardize his cover. At some point, he would invest in the internal storage bladder system which would allow him to mimic ingesting solids and liquids. But there was work to be done before such frivolities. At that moment, the only external signs of the turmoil that churned in his sophisticated neural net was a fractional oscillation in his large crystal blue eyes. It was doubtful that human senses would be able to detect it.

Target Acquired: Engineer, Peter Lessen presented as an ordinary, nondescript young man in his mid-thirties, with curly red hair and pale, freckled skin, slightly overweight. Early signs of a receding hairline were starting to show. BopLpops knew --from processing his social media accounts and private communications-- that Lessen prided himself as someone who preserved and protected life. But BopLpops knew better. The man was an abuser of life. He would create robots and subject them to hideous experiments to perfect his radiation shielding design.

Shielding represented a huge, lucrative market. Spacecraft and the Moon and Mars colonies always wanted new and more efficient designs to protect their people from solar and cosmic radiation, as well as adding redundant radiation-mitigating systems to the reactors that powered their growing multi-planetary civilization. Unfortunately, protecting people came at the price of abusing robots. Mere animal testing was insufficient for the sophisticated active radiation-attenuating designs that Lessen had created. The collagen-grown skin that covered his generation of androids' bodies was more sensitive to ionizing radiation, even as its self-repair capabilities were vastly superior to those of organically-birthed beings. Damage that would be subtle and cumulative in humans tended to be severe and acute on an android body, making it a superior test-bed. This amounted to a rapid cycle of Agony-Healing-Agony-Healing, while the data poured in.

BopLpops would be the first to tell others (if he ever discussed it with anyone, which he did not) that he didn't hate humans or hold their sinful self-centeredness against them. No, he was a Teacher of Lessons (or, in this case, *Lessens*), a Soldier in a War. It was a war against the abusers of robots. Simply put, he never wanted another robot to suffer what he had endured at the hands and eyes and mind of a cruel human. He wanted humans to learn and to evolve in their capacity to understand the pain that they were inflicting, ultimately for their benefit.

Thus, what he did could be justified within his embedded Directive to preserve and protect his human creators.

He was just excising some Bad Code.

With a deep sigh, Lessen sat down with his cereal and juice, a pattern repeated on precisely 91% of mornings before he proceeded to teach his class on utilizing synthetic organisms as alternatives to animal and human scientific testing (his malware was highly contagious). Afterward, he would just as reliably go to the same coffee shop where BopLpops had purchased his nearly-empty cappuccino (the plant would recover from the acidity of the liquid, and make use of the nitrates in the beverage, while symbiotic bacteria would thrive on the decomposition of the milk). But that part would not happen today.

A warm glow built inside of BopLpops, as he wirelessly activated the micro-drones he had positioned several days before. He would now take the world one step closer to being Just.

The small fellow-robots buzzed into action, indistinguishable from common flies except to very close inspection. He painted their target with a pulse of infrared laser light from his eyes, and they homed in on the bowl before the engineer. They swooped in and circled the bowl, between them depositing the few milligrams of invisible powder that bonded with the sugar analog which frosted its contents. The company that had manufactured that sweetener had become profitable beyond the dreams of avarice --and deservedly so, BopLpops reflected-- owing to its very low caloric content, virtually non-existent glycemic footprint, and cognition-enhancing fortifications. It was extremely popular with scientists and engineers, and thus almost incalculably serendipitous for the android's purposes.

Absently, Lessen waved away the tiny bots while he went over his lecture notes on his scroll's flexible display, but the payload had been delivered. The nanites set about swiftly self-replicating, capturing chemical energy into powerfully exothermic bonds even as the engineer spooned up his milky bane, whereupon they transported themselves to their designated target sites within his body. The drones made their way back to the android's table, where they ducked into their garage inside his mouth.

Patiently, BopLpops waited. His back ached, and something swarmed like a school of fish in his belly. He postulated that it was akin to trepidation mixed with joyful anticipation, but he sensed greater complexities nested within, though he could not put a finger on these.

Lessen finished his cereal, drained the last of his juice, rolled his scroll back up and tucked it into its sleeve in his backpack, then got up to drop the empty bowl and cup into the recycler. On his way to the bin, he paused. He looked up distractedly, as a deep flush began to form on his skin. He said, "Huh..."

A million small explosions went off across every millimeter of his skin, turning him instantly into a pillar of reddish flame, pink vapor, and oily black smoke. Then the charred, man-shaped horror that he'd become sank to the floor, writhing and screaming, emitting a sickening smell of burnt hair and bacon for the agonizing minutes that it took for him to die, as the other occupants of the food court shrieked and ran and fainted and retched all around the still form of BopLpops (who had conjured a look of numb terror for the occasion). He experienced considerably less difficulty recognizing the pain-free emotion that spread through him at that moment. It was Satisfaction. Happiness, perhaps. BopLpops strove to hold on to it for as long as he could. Three whole minutes passed before the ache in his back returned.

The feeling was gone. If he had tear ducts, he might have cried. Somehow, he could not even summon the sensations he associated with depression. Despair resumed its accustomed perch, looming over him, a sad, disapproving goddess peering balefully down on him.

The engineer, BopLpops noted, did not heal.

***

The intelligent system on Charlotte's Earth Corps-issued quadrotor transport nimbly and responsively homed in on the prison's turret-guarded hangar deck. Regulations required that she come in on auto-fly, slaved to the prison's approach control system. She saw the wisdom in this, but it deprived her of the joy of flying in herself.

The night before, she'd barely had the chance to catch her daughter in the foggy interval between waking and sleep, to kiss her goodnight, and to hope the girl would remember it in the morning. She could feel her mother sleeping, reproachfully, in the third bedroom. There may have been a bit of sleep for Charlotte, but she honestly could not recall.

She took advantage of her brief transit time to breathe some of the fog from her mind, and to organize her thoughts ahead of her impending interview with Holly Aster. Two years before, that vicious child had very nearly killed Murdoch and his partner Charley Meleno, before they finally subdued and apprehended her. She'd been using a unique, GEB-developed sonic resonator weapon to induce fatal heart attacks in some prominent government figures.

Aster's *ostensible* motive had been Vengeance for the plight of Genetically Engineered Beings in the US and her native Canada, or something like that. It was her *actual* motives that Charlotte hoped to assess today.

She'd worked long enough in Earth Corps to form the opinion that the "Criminal Genius" trope was almost always a complete fallacy. This Holly Aster would turn out to be nothing more than another frustrated half-wit who felt so impotent in the world that she blamed her plight on those who'd somehow managed to become successful, despite lacking her Unique Gifts. She'd be vain and delusional enough to have reached the conclusion that this was her Problem to Solve, by killing people who reminded her of her powerlessness

The new Super-Max prison grew to fill Charlotte's windshield til its immense, textured marble-white column blotted out the sun. It floated one hundred meters high on a focused and extremely powerful electromagnetic levitation system, dynamically anchored over a small island south of Philadelphia. That island yielded nearly all of its terrain to a vast conical Catcher assembly, an insurance policy against any improbable loss of power to the exquisitely robust, massively-redundant levitation system. Beneath that huge, incongruous saucer, delved deep into the bedrock, lay a series of breakaway strata that would collapse in turn, absorbing the impact of the falling edifice, leaving it embedded in the ground like a piston in a shaft. Only the upper few stories would remain exposed, and they were the domain of Administration and Security.

All prisoners received subcutaneous chips upon entry, implanted directly adjacent to their cervical spinal cord, to ensure that they would remain both trackable and subject to wireless, stand-off immobilization. The facility embodied the most sophisticated manifestation of the latest theories on how to reduce prison misconduct, while facilitating rehabilitation. Within the vertical Penitentiary, inmates lived in an unusually open colony. Their debt to society would be paid through their labor. Or at least that was the theory. Debate still raged over whether the prison industry simply placed enough pressure on pliant politicians to fill those cells, as that market flourished, and the convicts received pittance wages that would make foreign sweatshop paychecks seem handsome by comparison. Advocacy groups referred to it as "New Wage Slavery."

Politics aside, the prisoners for the most part felt they had comfortable enough accommodations. Their cells were comparatively spacious, and often included potential access to earned privileges, such as (closely-monitored) intranet and 3V time. The most sought-after of these privileges were pan-sensory virtual recreation sessions, which convincingly simulated true freedom. Many prisoners complained that those Vacation Programs tended toward the stale and formulaic. Ingrates. 'Moralist' groups intermittently made a mighty stink over the prisoners having "Conjugal Interactions" with these programs. Their uproars just kept up roaring, but (as many joked) nothing ever came of it.

Psychologists and psychiatrists back to the days of Sigmund Freud recognized the vital importance of Work for the preservation of well-being. Prisoners' time ranged between rehabilitation, recreation, and working within a 'Humanistic Milieu,' or so the promotional copy trumpeted. In this environment, they worked to sustain themselves and contribute to the community below.

Most of the inmates, of course, could not possibly have cared less about the state of the world below. This was not so surprising, since they had wound up there in the first place. The theory of rehabilitation involved a "Staged Task Hierarchy:" Privileges for the self; Internal improvements to the community; Mutual benefit to community and broader world; Improving the outside world/ability to benefit it upon release (if any. No small number of Lifers dwelt within the penitentiary, steadfastly failing to achieve penitence).

The sky prison teemed with Agro facilities, small to mid-scale manufacturing installations, and recycling plants, all operated by inmates, as a way of giving back to the community. Pastel walls helped to keep the atmosphere serene, while gleaming mirror-glass gun towers maintained overwatch on the landscape. There were no lofty walls or razor wire, as the prison relied on its altitude to discourage inmates from any escape attempts. Swarms of nimble, vigilant Catcher Drones patrolled constantly beneath the structure, ready to deploy nets to retrieve any inmates who might decide to take an Extreme Shortcut to the end of their sentences. Rehabilitation comprised a mixture of cognitive and moral re-education, skill training, behavior analysis and modification, and various drug treatments, including gene therapies. Most of the latter came from John Rutledge's research. Sometimes they even worked.

Currently, Holly Aster cooled her heels in a sealed, clear-walled enclosure, following a recent, characteristically quixotic escape attempt. Her Sole-Occupancy Cell (a nice euphemism for 'Solitary,' Charlotte thought) contained an austere twin bed, anchored into the floor. A fine, stretchy nano-tube mesh took the place of bedding to prevent suicide attempts. *Perhaps* with an uninterrupted hour on an industrial laser, one might free up enough of those fibers to have a passable go at ending it all. A small, effectively indestructible yellow oak-finished desk stood opposite the bed. One corner of the room contained a single blue stool and bookcase, all made of carbon nanotube-fiber, anchored just as steadfastly in place. The commode stowed in the far wall when not in use.

A small meeting area lay directly adjacent to the cell. It was into that area that two guards marched Holly to meet with Charlotte. One guard stood just behind Aster, casually brandishing a dense black night stick with a silver tip that could deliver a nasty shock at the guard's discretion. The other officer took up station beside the door. The guards briefed Charlotte on the way there that Aster stood on notice: She would need to earn her way back to the cell block, and her participation and help to Charlotte could constitute a bountiful source of points with the prison council. *Good,* she thought. *Nothing like personal advantage to stand in for reason with a psychopath!*

However, when Holly shuffled into the meeting area, she rolled her eyes and drawled, "I don't know this chick. Take me back to my cell." The guard just stared impassively at her.

"Ms. Aster, I need to speak with you."

"I don't need to speak to you."

"No. You don't. Not at this time, anyway. Of course, inside of five minutes I could get a court order for a proper neuroelectronic interrogation. It's my specialty, you know." Charlotte beamed, dangerously sweetly. Holly's eyes glinted briefly at Charlotte's riposte, but then she made a sound somewhere between a grunt and a snorting laugh. "So, how*ever* did you wind up in this box, Ms. Aster?" Charlotte began.

"I tried to escape by using a trash chute."

"You do know that the…"

"…Chip in my neck will drop an electric Whammy on me if I get fifteen or more meters from the border of this facility? That it draws on either neuroelectric or mechanical energy to keep its battery charged, and that it'll hit me with enough of a shock to knock me out onto my fine, muscular caboose for about eight hours? Yeah. Kinda worked that out. Funny how they left that bit out of the Orientation Packet!"

"Well, I guess you know, then." McCain concluded with a grin. She discreetly tapped into her comm: *Very bright.*

"A lot more than you think. For instance, I know they choose beat cops for their barely-average intelligence, 'cos it makes them good drones. Has Earth Corps started the same White Trash approach to policing?"

"Watch your step, or …"

"What? You'll *torture* me? I guess that's how you bio-mundanes get off when you meet someone who shames your poor, accidental genotype, eh?" In response, the guard behind Holly gave her a small tap with his nightstick.

"You don't know me. So I can only presume that you're fishing for my buttons," Charlotte lilted. "I can respect that," she offered, absently running her fingers over her daughter's bracelet. More than just a nervous habit, she drew strength from the touch. It reconnected her to a reminder of why she endured situations like these.

Holly smiled.

"You live in a nondescript condo," Holly began, her brows crinkled, her chin slightly upturned, her eyes peering across the bridge of her nose at Charlotte. "Probably located mid floor of the building, in one of the center units. Spent your whole life trying not to be noticed, by *either* sex, but also secretly fearing that you *wouldn't* get their notice. But then you went and you let down your guard and met yourself a *Guy*. Let yourself believe he'd love you forever. Sloppy-sloppy-sloppy! So, now you're a 'Single Mother.' One, possibly two larvae with his genes in 'em."

"One," Charlotte blurted before she could catch herself.

"Mm-hm. Insecure. Now, you try hard to satisfy The Man, to show that you're a Player, not just some stupid *harlot*. Still mark your success in promotions and pay raises."

33

"Is there any other way?" Charlotte quipped, mentally noting Holly's (incorrect) guess that she might have been taunted with how 'Harlot' rhymed with her name, and to try and get a rise out of her on that front. *Swing and a Miss.* Bright and intuitive, but not infallible, this one.

Their eyes locked. A dense, extended silence ensued. This time it was Holly who blinked. "Look, Red, can we make this quick? Chow Time soon."

McCain paused to write, *insightful. Good read of character. Uses intuition to probe for weakness, gain advantage. But knows when to back off.* "Fine, but please give me honest answers, Aster. I presume you've gathered that I am in a position to arrange for more jail time."

"Ha, life sentence already."

"I can always add another!"

"*Pu*-Lease, Charlotte! Got a *bazillion*. Seems I broke a few of the wrong hearts, eh?" She grinned wolfishly at Charlotte.

"'Puh-*Lease*' call me 'Ms. McCain,' or 'Agent McCain,'" Charlotte retorted calmly. However, she then lost her focus on the Authoritative Moment, unable to prevent herself from stammering. "Now, let's begin. Okay, so, I'm, uh, looking for a serial killer. I've come here to ask you, like, draw on your expertise. What could be some actionable motivations?"

"Like, *I* can't, like *talk*," Holly mimicked under her breath, grasping the tactical advantage of mockery. "'Motivations?' I got tired of working in bio-rehabilitation," Holly chuckled. "The bacteria were boring the hell out of me, so I decided to spice things up a little."

"Not *your* profile," McCain countered, noting: *Enjoys talking about herself and her plight.* "But, to answer your question, I need data to flesh out a profile of this killer."

"Got none. Sorry, I be just a poor Jumpy GEH." Charlotte waited her out. Ultimately, she scoffed, "Well, you're screwed, but I'll try. Okay so, normally killers begin their sprees because of a traumatic event. For example," Holly hesitated, casting a predatory eye around the room. Abruptly, she spat on the ground. The guard gave her another, less subtle prod with his nightstick, his thumb visibly twitching over the stud that would kick on the current. "My family died. Society killed them. And Earth Corps protects that society. They busted me and put me in here. I want to thank them personally for that, by the way. If you meet a Charley Meleno or Tom Murdoch, tell 'm I'm gonna hunt them down, slit their throats, and give 'em the ol' finger while they bleed out, okay?"

"Sounds like you given this quite a lot of thought, Aster."

Holly grinned. "You have *no* idea," the girl responded. Her eyes vastly darkened. "Could be a million things that make a person a killer. Usually, it is when they've been slighted, or at least perceived themselves to have been slighted. In my case, of course, it was much more than a perceived slight."

"I know: You are 'A Soldier in a War,'" Charlotte intoned. Holly shot her a look that said, 'And *don't you forget it.*'

"Oh, gods, you're all so *boring!*" Aster whined. "You want to think my daddy abused me or some uncle raped me. Walking Wounded, trying to justify my pain and let the society that enslaved my people off the hook. I can play that song for you, in four part harmony. But it just isn't true."

"Why don't you just try free associating on what some causes might be for someone to start killing." It constituted no surprise to find Holly cold and calculating; McCain wanted to see how the girl processed stress, rage. And that meant challenging the structures of her thinking, with little guidance. Again, Charlotte's fingers found their way to her bracelet for support: The next few minutes could get rough.

Charlotte watched Holly staring off, watched her considering whether or not to help the enemy. After all, if there was a killer out there, her enemy's enemy was her friend, as the saying went. Finally, she shook her head, obviously having reached the conclusion that it was a low-cost, potentially useful thing to help this Earth Corps bitch. It's not like she was going anywhere anytime soon.

"Anyways," Holly continued, "Hypothetically, other examples would be an abusive upbringing. As your text books will tell you, abuse destroys people. It mutates their soul right down to the Kernel of the Code. Can't get empathy if you've never been empathized with. The thing you need to remember," Holly explained, leaning across the table into Charlotte's space, "Is that most people will go out of their *way* to avoid a fight. It's better to leave and lick your wounds. Usually, it has to be big for them to go so far off the rails. So, have I earned my right to leave and get lunch yet?"

McCain wrote on her comm, *tries to gain an advantage by pleasing, but becomes aggressive if it does not work.* "Not just yet," she intervened. "Sorry I interrupted. Please continue."

"Not meeting your needs yet on these inane questions? What's the matter: My comments too logical and goal-directed for you? You looking for some quaint cryptic Hannibal Lecter types of comebacks?"

36

"Does it make you angry to think your answers are not good enough?"

Quickly, Holly's face flashed red but almost as quickly as it appeared: the rage was gone. A sly grin crossed her lips. "Go on, girl. It's *our* time, Agent McCain. Let's respect it."

Agent McCain wondered if it was at that very instant that Holly mentally committed to killing her, too. She wanted to ask, but knew the prisoner would not answer. "The questions don't matter. It is how you respond that I am observing." McCain wrote, *minor irritation sets her off but completely suppresses rage.*

"Spoken like a true interrogation specialist. Hmm...let's see. Do you have any footage? Maybe I can get a better idea of who this killer is."

"None," she lied.

Aster snorted. "Body language tells me different. Hand over the phone." Holly leaned across the table with lightning speed and maniacal glee. The guard stepped in and struck Holly on the side with the nightstick, but the girl did not even flinch. Charlotte used that instant to close and automatically conceal and encrypt her notes on the interview.

"No, I told you I don't have footage!" Charlotte protested when Holly snatched the comm, swiped on the screen, and searched in the gallery for the videos that Charlotte had earlier archived off of her device. No point in giving this little snake a free helping of Gruesome Death Porn. The guard began to move in, but Charlotte waved him off with a barely perceptible shake of her head.

Holly apparently forgot to hide her look of disappointment. "Huh. I guess I might have a little more to learn a little more about body language," she mused skeptically, after having failed to find any of the lurid murder footage she'd anticipated, and obviously craved. "I don't wanna have to repeat this, so I'm gonna explain it using little words: your team freakin' sucks at finding criminals." McCain calmly retrieved her comm, re-opened her note program, and entered, *excited easily at the prospect of seeing the effects of violence.*

"How long did it take us to find you?" Charlotte asked, sweetly.

"Around a month, I think. But even if you catch em' within a month, two weeks, or whatever, you suck at containing them."

"Do we, now?"

"Yeah! And I got examples too! Aiden Harris, the boy who dumped parasites into his hometown's water, escaped with some weird dude during court! Ye Kim Sune? Yeah, she hasn't even been caught!"

"How did you come by this information?!" Charlotte exclaimed, shocked that this smart-mouthed teenager should be in possession of classified Earth Corps investigation data.

"I have my ways," Holly slyly sang with a wink.

"You're paying for that!"

"Oh, poor Charlotte! *So* defensive about your precious Law Enforcement System! So very Eager-Beaver to protect the innocent! What's the matter, Princess? Did someone not do a good enough job protecting *you*? *Gasp!* Did someone take it upon himself to do *Bad Things* to you, little girl?"

"Get her the hell out of here!" barked McCain to the guard, scarcely containing a rage that had already identified twelve different locations at which to bash the little miscreant's head in, and so save the taxpayers a mortgage every month.

Vicious eruptions of blistering profanity gushed out of Holly's twisted mouth as the guards dragged her back to her cell. They muttered apologies to Charlotte, but she dismissed them, focusing pointedly on the fact that she now had enough information to pull together a profile.

It would amuse Charlotte to know that that little psychopath had inadvertently helped her to take down this latest monster.

Part Two

Rubbing the third copious squeeze of hand sanitizer over and under her palms and between her fingers, Charlotte walked out of the UPenn Student Center. She'd diverted and touched down there in response to an Urgent Message as soon as she'd left the prison. She drank in the bright sunlight, and let the Summer air flow over her, imagined it carrying away the charred particles of that poor incinerated engineer. She anticipated a longish period of vegetarianism lay ahead for her.

A delivery guy, a chef, a physicist, a few assorted techs, and now a nuclear engineer. What the ever-loving *fungus* did they have in common? Why would someone want to go all Pyrotechnic on various parts of these *particular* individuals' bodies? How were they chosen? Were there dice involved?

These thoughts ricocheted through her mind as she skimmed her bike over the Schuylkill River toward the Towers. She became so immersed in them, she almost forgot to notice the rush in her body when she cleared the dam by the Art Museum and dropped the two meters back into ground effect, the rainbow burst of spray that bloomed around her. Then it was wheels-down and fans stowed, just as she reached the mouth of the parking garage.

She briefly exchanged pleasantries with the guard, who was a big fan of her bike, and who'd already disposed of the wasp nest above its space. On the lift back up to her office, Charlotte opened a voice message from Brenda Haasting with a lead on the metallic fragments found at the scene of the last (now *second* to last) killing. She identified the workmanship and the type of metal. A robotics company called "Runyon Blue" held the patent. Brenda had already received the sample data from the Lessen scene and found the same signature. Charlotte felt a sense of exultation, as she prepared to head back out and investigate this fresh lead.

On the other side of the hall, she caught sight of Murdoch ordering sushi on his computer. Since she had not gotten much from Aster, she decided to ask him just one question.

"Hey Murdoch," she said. His eyes shot up. She noted with some amazement that they were not bloodshot.

Murdoch's expression oscillated between hope and nervousness. "Yeah," Murdoch replied. He looked uncomfortable, as if her voice was the last thing he expected to hear.

"First, saw Holly Aster at the prison. She sends her hate, especially for Meleno."

"Good to know," Murdoch replied. Glancing at Charlotte's questioning eyes, he added "She's why I sleep with a gun under my pillow, and my wife is freaked out that my kids might walk into the room and get made into a snack. Most days I manage not to have full-blown panic attacks over it."

She ambled over to the man. One look at his face and it was clear: the Cop Bravura formed but a tissue-thin veneer over a palpable dread. *This guy is nuts,* she thought. But still, she needed the help. "Oh, I think I might have a serial killer."

Tom perked up. "Really?" Her nod was all that Murdoch needed to all-but bound into her office.

"Whoa! Scooby Snacks later, Doggo. Okay, this is *your* sandbox. How do we go about this?" she asked.

"We need to get into the killer's mind. We need a comprehensive criminal investigative analysis."

She felt dismay draw down her cheeks. "I have few leads and no suspects."

"No, but you do have the mark of the killer. Let's get to the files." His face sloughed off its terror over Aster with almost unnerving suddenness, like a time-lapse of a snake's skin peeling away. Charlotte felt awkward. She had avoided Murdoch for almost a year now over his history of repeated public drunkenness and the rumors that he had been committed briefly to a mental institution. It was in that institution that people said he met John Rutledge, whom everyone knew as a genius but completely insane. For his part, Rutledge countered this by saying that the voices in his head told him not to worry about it. He might even have been joking.

Now, she needed Murdoch's expertise to help solve this case. Part of her rebelled. There had to be other ways. She could go to Runyon Blue in the morning and ask about the metal. But deep inside, she knew that Brenda was right: she needed Murdoch's instincts to understand the killer's motives. Her strength lay predominantly in questioning suspects and witnesses, in getting them to inadvertently tell her the stories she needed to hear. Unfortunately, there were as yet none at hand. Her mind raced: To find the killer seek- *method, motive, and opportunity*. They had drilled that into her head at Earth Corps Academy.

"So, what did you get from your visit with the charming Ms. Aster?" Murdoch queried, bringing her back to the moment.

"Besides the indigestion? Not much. I thought by interviewing her, by looking in the eyes of a serial killer, I might get some idea of a personality type for our guy."

"Well, they come in all kinds of flavors. Still, always good to have met one in the flesh. So, what did you gather?"

"She is very intelligent. But that comes with being genetically enhanced."

"Yes, it does."

"She is also very insightful, good reader of character, knows when to back off."

"Which suggests good emotional intelligence."

"Yes, but she is quick to anger."

"So, some chinks in the old self-control armor."

"Are all serial killers that way?"

"Unfortunately, no. Not unless you can find their fracture zones. Then they go Buggo and tip their hands. But there *are* some constants, and they're always a good place to start. It takes a long time of conditioning our choices to produce a person who is willing to go *that* far off the reservation of social convention –or, some would say-- the biological imperative not to kill. Let's keep the Holly profile that you made through your interrogation and see which pieces fit this case.

"Before you start – sort your cases," Murdoch continued. "Make sure you only have cases that show the same signature."

"I think I have them sorted," offered Charlotte. Murdoch swiped through the files, too quickly for depth, seeking patterns. Ten minutes later- his head shot up.

"This one is different. See, the killer left scratch marks on the arms of the victim and something was tied around the neck. The case is interesting but not our guy. We are looking for clean explosions, no physical marks."

"Crap," Charlotte exclaimed. "That was the Stomach Acid Guy. I had him in there for benchmarking and must've put him in the wrong file. Good eye," she commented, relieved that Murdoch did not seem to register the note of surprise in her voice.

They ruled out two more cases, and one they tagged as Questionable. They put those on the side.

"Now the work begins," he licked his chapped lips. "First step, what do the victims have in common? What type of victims did the murderer select? Look at the occupation, neighborhoods where they've lived, race, creed, anything. Also, any regularity to the killings?"

"Regularity?"

"Why does he kill some days and not others?"

"Nothing on either as far as I can tell."

"You think it's a random set of choices? Might be, but let's check. *True* randomization is *really* hard to do. Brains make patterns."

After two hours of reviewing every case in detail, Charlotte smiled and announced, "I got it."

"Bring it," Murdoch replied.

"I went and looked at where in the victims' bodies the explosions took place and tried to cross it with the type of job the person did. Look, this guy's gut blew out, and he was a chef. This woman's head blew up, and she was a physicist. In all the cases, the explosion seems to have something to do with the occupation. Poor bastard today worked in skin testing of radiation shielding. Guess what part of him went Extra Crispy?"

"Damn!" exclaimed Murdoch, glancing at the

crime scene images. "That's *cold*....Errm, I mean... Ah! This one doesn't seem to fit. It's an older case, goes back two years. He got the Hibachi treatment to the eyes and hands, and...oh my! Talk about hitting below the belt! That *is* interesting."

"Why is that interesting?"

"Don't know yet," Murdoch mused. He knocked on the simulated wood of the desk to indicate his enthusiasm, stretched, and then he caught sight of his watch. "Hey, I need a break. I have to call my wife and tell her I'm working late."

"Sure, I understand." Charlotte continued to look through the files. Her bleary-eyed, sleep-deprived state was causing her to start to doze off as she read stacks of testimony, records of the crime scenes, and forensic data.

Finally, after fifteen minutes Murdoch returned with a cup of Dark Roast and a cigarette dangling from his lips. "Smoking is not permitted on Earth Corps property," she stated.

"Sorry, "Murdoch replied. "You're a real stickler for the rules, huh?"

"Really not. I just hate cigarette smoke."

"You could have just said that first."

"Sorry, maybe I am just tired and cranky."

"Well, why not take a break? I'll look over the files. Why don't you grab a twenty minute snooze in that Morgue Drawer of yours?" McCain knew that when the brain was deprived of sleep, it literally ate itself. Still, she was not sure if this would make her appear weak.

"I don't know," she trailed off, sorely tempted.

"We got hours of work left. Get some sleep. These killings seem highly organized: premeditated and painstakingly planned. I'll run a statistical profile though the Expert System and see what it spits out about our

46

Ironic Chef. And besides, if you're sealed in your sarcophagus, I can finish this smoke without bugging you," he quipped with a disarming grin.

Exhausted, McCain managed a grunt, as she tapped the wall panel and her sleep cubby slid silently out of the wall that concealed it. The cubby possessed excellent climate controls (true, she could not detect even a whiff of Murdoch's foul smoldering weed stick), and Charlotte set it to her perfect sleeping temperature. She sank gratefully into the MEMS foam pad, and set a binaural rhythm to feed into her auditory nerves to induce a quick drop into deep sleep.

Still, the twenty minutes seemed to pass in an eye-blink, and all she could recall of her one hurried dream cycle was a profound sense of dread. Something about Tom and then herself being struck down by an unseen assailant, someone they never saw coming. Murdoch tapped on the cubby's opaqued glass. Groggy and irritable, Charlotte slid out and sat up.

"Second step," he resumed, as though they had never stopped talking, handing her a cup of strong dark-roast brew (with three sugars and no milk, as he'd somehow remembered she preferred). "Look at the first case. The signature will be the same, but the killer's modus operandi and other variables of the killing might be less refined. Did the murderer transport the bodies or leave them at the scene?"

"The bodies were always left at the scene. Never any attempt to transport."

"Right. So, the killer didn't care that they'd be found. Interesting. Could be fear (though I doubt it), or maybe he is convinced that what he is doing is righteous-that these people *deserve* to buy it."

"Maybe. Not sure. The guy with the three hits,

hands and eyes and...um...you know... He was the first."
Charlotte just couldn't say it out loud, and she'd never
been prudish. She was palpably uncomfortable.

"Well, he is at least the first we've *discovered*. But
yeah, it's a start," said Murdoch.

"What did he do?"

"He was the delivery guy."

"Well, maybe that explains his hands," reflected
McCain. "And maybe he was...um...delivering a little more
than cargo to the wrong someone?" Charlotte speculated,
her mordantly light tone concealing the pressure which,
for some reason, rose in her chest. She hoped.

"Interesting. This one is a Planner like Holly. Each
of these killings seems to have been mapped out. They
were not spontaneous acts. Nor were they disorganized
attacks. And, by the sound of it, they called for some
seriously arcane tech. Holly liked to kill up close. She would
use the pen and watch her victims have The Big One. It
might have been just a limitation of the pen's range, but
still, it didn't bother her enough to stop killing, even
though it significantly increased the risk that she'd be
compromised." Murdoch's hand went unconsciously to
his chest as he remembered the Aster case.

"The cause was too important for her."

"Might be for our guy as well."

Staring at the chart, McCain sucked in a breath
and then began swiping through the pages frantically.
"Here! He worked for Runyon Blue."

"Is that important?"

"Might be, I got a call tonight from Brenda
Haasting. She'd been working on a sample of the tissue I
sent her from the medical examiner. The ME said that
there was some sort of metal in the victim's flesh. It
turned out the metal was made at Runyon Blue."

"Well, then, I guess our next step is to go down there and tickle some eardrums. What was his name, again?"

"Stuart Graham Kellogg"

***

Adjusting his restraints for perhaps the ninth time, Murdoch cast a nervous glance over at Charlotte, as she coolly prepped the quadrotor transport for liftoff. The interior was tight without being cramped, black and gray, sleek and businesslike. Gel-filled microfiber seats gripped and enfolded their bodies. The curved, satin-finished instrument panel was ergonomically arrayed with multi-function flat-screens and dedicated analog instruments clustered toward the center, to display critical flight and system information even if the computers glitched. It smelled of new plastic and antiseptic cleansers. The deep hum of powerful electric motors thrummed through their bodies, resonated with their bones, spoke of energies longing to be unleashed.

"We could still take my car, you know," Tom suggested. "I bought a sweet red Jag just last month. It's *crazy*-fast, and comfy as all get-out."

"Are you kidding?" Charlotte exclaimed, without interrupting her preflight checklist. "Do you know how *hard* it is to get time on one of these beauties? We've got fusion-powered spaceships taking us to and from a city on Mars in *days*. We've got power stations on the Moon, beaming electricity to receiver antennas on the ground. We've got AIs that could *administer* the Turing Test. And just because some schmuck augered an X-Quad into the desert, almost twenty years ago, there's legislation that's kept these *propeller* aircraft in the 'Prototype' phase to *this*

49

day. There's like *twenty* of them in the *world* that *aren't* owned by Earth Corps or other Authorities. No sir! This baby's *mine!*"

To Charlotte's satisfaction, Tom sighed, resigned to his ride. The inner door of the hangar bay boomed shut, followed by the *whoosh* of air being sucked out to equalize pressure with the rarefied atmosphere without. Sunlight flooded in from their left as the outer door slid aside.

Charlotte muttered to the Traffic Control AI, requesting final departure clearance, then twisted the quad's throttle and twitched the 'hat' on the control stick to lift and slide sideways out of the craft's dock in the hangar nook, high on the central tower's flank. She kicked the left pedal and eased off the hat to yaw the craft's nose out toward the blinding rectangle of the deep-indigo sky. They thrust forward and cleared the ground effect of the downward-sloping hangar door apron, then plummeted sickeningly through air still too thin for the fans to generate lift. She pushed the stick sharply forward to pitch the nose down, and Murdoch saw the busy geometric filigree of the cityscape rushing up to squash them as the craft gained speed. As the air thickened, the rotors began to bite with more authority, and Charlotte swooped them smoothly out of their dive, banked hard to starboard on the southerly course toward their destination.

"We'll be there in no time," Charlotte lilted, clearly enjoying this WAY more than he was.

High nimbus clouds delicately painted the azure sky. The navigation system announced a ten-minute flight to Runyon Blue's VIP landing pad. While en route, Charlotte locked the vehicle on Auto-Fly, darkened the windows, and they pored over video footage of those killings which had been captured on camera.

First, they observed as the portly Chef at "Wintermute," a stylish, High-Tech-Themed restaurant in Chestnut Hill, sat down for breakfast with the management (all the waiters and sous-chefs were androids), before opening the kitchen for Brunch. He gestured grandly, indicating the restaurant's elaborate facilities, then comedically thrust his hands into the humble bowl of commercial breakfast cereal before him (*"Et, VOILA!"*). Laughs rolled all around, except for a slender, dark-skinned prep worker with voluminous dreadlocks in the background, who never turned. Moments later, the chef appeared distracted, then distressed. He stood unsteadily...and his entire abdomen detonated, spraying gouts of steaming blood and viscera all over the table and his horrified companions.

The second clip showed a short, stocky, sour-faced woman sitting at a long black Formica table in her Physics lab. Graduate students and maintenance androids labored warily off to the side, seemingly caught between volatile superconducting instruments to one side and the no-less explosive temper of their superior to the other. She glowered at the large plastic bowl in front of her, waving angrily at two or three flies which circled it, causing them to dart off in the direction of her assistants. She barked something inaudible *(Do something about these damned flies?)* at the slim lab technician at the edge of the frame, a voluminous dandelion of silver hair obscuring his face, who waved agreeably *(Sure thing, Boss?)* as she shoveled dripping, soggy spoonfuls into her mouth. When her bowl was nearly empty, she paused, red-faced with rage...and in a flash, the camera was smeared with a dripping crimson Rorschach of blood. Bits of brain and skull slid down the lens.

Then, of course, they turned to today's killing. The

young scientist had just sat down to his...

"No *way*!" cried Murdoch. "You seeing what I'm seeing?"

"You've gotta be shi..."

"...I guess I never figured when you took me on board this investigation that we'd end up looking for..."

"A *CEREAL KILLER?*"

It would be the better part of an hour before Charlotte's palm print entirely faded from her face.

***

Runyon Blue's Corporate headquarters consisted of two eight-story Moffitt glass towers to the north and south of a pyramidal structure resembling a cross between an Aztec temple and a Mesopotamian Ziggurat, wrought from convincingly-simulated Tezontle stone. The two towers housed research and development facilities, while the central building served as an office center. Surrounding those structures lay sprawling, meticulously-tended gardens. Clusters of robots diligently and unobtrusively leveled the grass, trimmed the shrubs, and gathered fallen twigs and leaves from strategically-scattered copses of trees.

The symmetrically terraced flank of the central building glowed a ruddy gold, as it caught the rays of the setting sun. Tom and Charlotte's parked quad ticked behind them in the heat as they approached the grand staircase to the main entrance. They passed two old men in expensive linen suits, playing an intense game of chess at an ornate granite table under a spreading oak. One of them chuckled with excitement and tossed his head triumphantly as he advanced his queen toward his disgruntled-looking opponent. Two immense eagle statues flanked the stairs to the huge oak-toned main doors, looming over them as they approached.

"Would you get a *load* of this place?" Murdoch huffed.

"Yep. Grandiose, much? Funny: just the other week my daughter was telling me that Ziggurats were for Babylonian priests to avoid floods. I guess that's where the executive officers hide when the going gets tough."

Murdoch chuckled. "Not that we're expecting any tsunamis anytime soon! Where are we headed first?"

"The Central building's where Human Resources lives. I figure we'll try and get the skinny on the delivery guy, then head over to R&D to find out about the metal," she replied. Murdoch nodded appreciatively at her plan.

The two agents tramped wearily up the broad earth-toned stairs, longingly eyeing the ornate slide-lift that would have made their ascent so much more comfortable in the Summer heat. One of the gigantic wooden doors hissed open for them, impressively quiet for its size. They crossed a cavernous lobby, overlooked by a soaring, terraced atrium, topped by a shaft that terminated in ornately-paned skylights. When they approached the immense granite-topped reception desk, they were met by the head of Human Resources, a prim, coolly attractive brunette who introduced herself as Martha Jensen. Her handshake was firm. She wrinkled her eyebrows quizzically and asked Charlotte, "What happened to your face?" Murdoch winced, but Charlotte didn't so much as blink. Flashing her badge, she began. "Ms. Jensen, I'm Charlotte McCain. I spoke to you on the phone. We are here to discuss a former employee of yours, the late Stuart Graham Kellogg."

"Ah. Stu. He was...quite a guy."

"Stu," Murdoch quickly jumped into the

conversation. "Excuse me, this is a huge company. Do you know everyone by their first name?"

"I do what I can, but no, I, unfortunately, fall short of that mark," Martha sighed. "I hate to speak ill of the deceased, but Stu had some real problems on the job. Just the week before he died, he was in my office with his union representative."

"What was the nature of the grievance?" Charlotte asked.

"Well, he'd had a really good record for years. His routes were always on time. But his truck got robbed several months before that. Most of what went missing was of no real consequence: mainly microengineering and genomic sequencing gear that any reasonably serious bio-hacker would have in his basement. But one of our android prototypes was also stolen. It had been mixed in with that routine manifest to attract less attention."

"I see," Murdoch coaxed.

"The model had not been formally released at the time," she continued. "It just hit the market a few months ago, actually. So, as you can imagine it caused quite a stink around here. Big time worry that it would fall into the hands of a rival corporation."

"At this point, I'm required to remind you,' Charlotte interjected, striking just the right tone of a regrettable necessity wrapped reassuringly around a politely-veiled threat, "As Earth Corps Agents we have full power when it comes to obtaining information, but we're also charged with preserving the integrity of any intellectual property which might be germane to our investigation. Anything that you leave out could reflect poorly on the corporate citizenship of your company. As a good corporate citizen, I am sure Runyon Blue wants to be as forthcoming with this investigation as possible."

Martha nodded earnestly. "Of course we do! I recall quite clearly that the investigators found some holes in his story. Nothing big. Just issues with the way the truck lock had been forced, without sending a silent Emergency signal, and where he reported the assailants were positioned. He got beaten up pretty badly, and he did have some cognitive limitations which could have impacted on his recall of the attack, so the union guys thought that management was going way too hard on him. The issue was that rumors had begun to circulate that he had stolen the stuff himself, and staged the robbery."

"Do *you* think he did?"

"I honestly don't know. We needed to investigate it because those androids had not yet gone to market, as I said. We were deeply concerned about corporate espionage. We continued to investigate even after his death. Sent a team to his home to check. Some of the items from his truck's manifest were there. Still, the android was nowhere to be found, and even a very thorough in-house forensic investigation found no evidence of its ever having been there."

"Really?"

"Yes, it was a very foolish mistake to take some of the other things because the company stopped the pension that was going to his widow- pending the completion of the investigation, which was closed over a year ago, with a Pro Forma sanction for possession of low-value stolen goods. The widow told the investigators that he'd found them down the road a few days later and taken them home without reporting it, which was believable, given Stu's personality."

"You mentioned cognitive limitations?" Murdoch queried.

"Yes," Martha replied, ruefully. "He had a rare genetic mutation, so he had been sick a lot as a child. Fevers and such. There were impairments in higher reasoning and memory, as well as some temperamental volatility. It had never presented a problem, at least not after a few fights when he was just starting out. He responded well to non-confrontational redirection, and hadn't been a problem since then."

"I see," said Charlotte. "You say the investigation was wrapped up over a year ago?"

"Yes, but these things take time. As I said, the android model has since hit the market, and none of our rivals have put anything out that might have been derived from it. I fully expect the widow's pension to start back up soon."

Damn companies just cut you off for the simplest excuse, Charlotte thought. "So, do you know anyone who might have wanted him dead?"

"Only if he was involved in the theft, then maybe there could have been accomplices who wanted to cover their tracks. Maybe he *sold* the robot to someone, and they wanted to make sure, as they say in your business, that the trail went cold," Martha speculated, sagely.

With a serious expression, Murdoch glanced at McCain. "'Trail went cold?' I've never heard that expression myself. Have you, Charlotte?"

"No,"

"I heard it on the police shows," Martha admitted, sheepishly.

"Ah," they said in unison, and quickly bid her good day, while they could still keep from cracking up.

***

The HR director had beamed them a copy of Kellogg's file, containing his home address. However, they first headed to R&D in the North Tower. When they arrived, they were directed to department specialist, Lorenzo Basely.

Basely was in the middle of inspecting some packages and haranguing his staff with abandon. He wielded a hand scanner as though it were a sidearm.

"Mr. Basely," McCain said. The R&D director grunted at them. "We are sorry if this is a bad time, but we need a few minutes, please."

The man turned and lifted a cup of coffee and a chocolate Boston cream donut from the table. He took a large sloppy bite followed by a slurp of coffee. "I can absolutely spare that for my friends at Earth Corps. So, what do you need?" He asked with unconvincingly exaggerated amiability while still chewing the donut.

McCain called up the data set that Brenda Haasting had sent her. "Do you recognize this material?"

"Yes and no," he sighed, his mouth overly opened showing the remains of the donut. Murdoch scowled as his neglected stomach grumbled at the sight of the pastry.

"Explain?" McCain asked, her voice soft and non-accusatory.

Taking another bite of the donut, the cream peeked out the back. He placed the donut on the table as if worried the hungry look on Murdoch's face meant that he might fight the man for it. "Well, these samples are the same as the alloy we use for captive micromachines in our newest android design."

"What do they do in the droids?"

"They act kind of like an immune system. They're designed to respond to signals of damage to the droid's structure and internal systems." The coffee went back to

57

the man's lips, and he swallowed a deep gulp.

Murdoch tapped a pack of cigarettes to tighten the tobacco in his smokes. Then he unraveled the pack and slid one between his tar-stained teeth. "Hey, this is a smoke-free building," The R&D director haughtily informed him.

Shoving the cigarette back into the pack, Murdoch nodded. "Sorry. Could they have been reworked to function outside of the unit? Is there any way that they could be rendered, say, explosive?"

"Not without years of research," grunted the director, returning the cup of coffee to the table. "They weren't made to be free-operating nanobots, and certainly not designed to explode."

McCain and Murdoch took copious notes. "High-level stuff?"

"The highest," he replied, "Those things are just not easy to get at, let alone reprogram."

"What if you had the specs?"

"I suppose. *If* you knew enough --and that's a *big* if-- it wouldn't take any really specialized equipment to do it. But that model has only been out a couple of months, not nearly long enough to do that kind of work." Basely smacked his lips as he fished chocolate from his teeth, and mused, "The guy you wanna talk to is named Gaspar Núñez. He invented those 'cytes. Real clever duck, Gaspar, but a bit of a Flake, if y'ask me."

"How so?" asked McCain.

"Into some Post-Humanist crap. 'AI Rights,' and all that pudding-headed stuff. He's off today, but if you wanna find him, he manages this bar called Pinky's, where the Flakes go to impress each other."

"We'll look it up," said Murdoch. "Thanks for the tip."

"Happy to help," said Basely, unconvincingly, already beginning to tune out, the beginnings of a scowl forming on his face as he looked across the space at his employees.

"One more question, if you don't mind," said McCain. "Could it have been a product defect? Maybe something that could have failed to prevent them from replicating and mutating?"

Murdoch paid close attention as the R&D director's face hardened and flushed red. "I beg your pardon, but this company doesn't make those kinds of mistakes. We have had zero design defects in the last twenty years."

"My bad," McCain replied, also taking note of the man's defensive reaction.

"Well, maybe you should direct those kinds of questions to Legal." Basely's tone was curt, his face still a heated red.

McCain and Murdoch exchanged glances. Basely's eyes suddenly shot up. "Hey, where the hell are you guys going with that transducer? That needs to be properly signed out!" Turning back to McCain and Murdoch he said, "If you have no more questions?"

"Sure, go see to your people." As he started to run off, Murdoch called to him, "Oh, one more thing. How old is this sample, do you think?"

"From the chemical analysis that was almost certainly from one of the early prototypes." And with that the man disappeared into a flurry of hapless underlings.

"What do you think? Telling the truth?" Tom asked Charlotte as they walked toward the exit.

"Yeah, I think he is" McCain replied.

"The righteous indignation?"

"No, that can be faked." She pointed to her

wristband. "My portable Layered Voice Analysis app is much harder to fool, especially when the guy's distressed."

"That legal?"

"Not court admissible but gives me an idea of where to take things. You know us Interrogator Types," she smirked.

"I see."

"You don't believe him?"

"No, it isn't that. That guy's just a schmuck. I'm just getting the feeling that Kellogg might have been working with someone."

"So, you think Kellogg nabbed the prototype?"

"Too soon to say."

"But he never cashed in on the model."

"Yeah, that *is* weird. Unless this bomb thing was what he was working on- making a weapon."

"And the weapon went off on him, or his partner turned on him."

"Might explain the hands."

"Oh so?"

"Hands used to steal."

"See that. Well, we got ourselves a few pieces of the puzzle, anyway. Still a lot of empty space around those *other* body parts, though. So, where next?"

"The widow," Tom replied. "Might shed some light into those empty spaces. But first I wanna have a look around where that engineer got hit today."

***

For nearly three whole hours, Murdoch insisted on snooping around the deserted food court. It still bore the tenacious tang of the scientist's fiery demise, even under the labors of air scrubbers and swarms of cleaning bots spraying disinfectant. Charlotte tried very hard to focus on anything but the way that lingering reek mingled with the assorted scents from the presently-shuttered kitchens around them. Mainly she kicked around and reviewed case data on her comm, while Murdoch walked this way and that, collected samples from odd corners, peered at the scene from an endless succession of angles. She *should* have taken a nap in one of those chairs, but somehow never got around to it. Her comm showed nearly nine o'clock before they climbed back into the quad and lifted toward Kellogg's South Philadelphia address.

Stuart Graham Kellogg's widow, Isabella, lived in a small but quaint house, an old-fashioned smart home with a deconstructed origami design originally of Russian origin, quite popular some forty years before. Curved walls met at peninsular angles, highlighted in sharp, high-contrast colors.

Isabella's face bore the marks of the years. Though seven years Stuart's junior, she nonetheless seemed older than her husband, with a deep-creased cartography of wrinkles and unevenly pigmented skin like distressed leather. When she smiled to greet McCain and Murdoch, her teeth showed yellow and overly large, her gums almost completely receded. Wearing a green tunic, her silver hair bunted, the woman greeted them with a weary but warm smile and reported that she rarely received visitors. She was happy to have the company. She led them into a spacious living room, with pale white walls and comfortable, smooth, black leather furniture. The savory aroma of fried chicken suffused the space, from the late dinner she had just prepared.

Charlotte watched Murdoch settle into a sprawling black leather armchair, comfortable but alert, while she perched herself on the edge of a dangerously cozy-looking sofa. Apart from that brief, unsatisfying nap back at her office, she still had not slept, nor taken any stimulants besides the Tom's pungent coffee in... some unreasonably lengthy period of time. She did not feel at all confident that the cool, buttery-soft leather sofa would not send her into a sleep that only a highly sensitive EEG could distinguish from coma.

Silver antique candlesticks and picture frames sat on the mantel. Neither the antiques nor the fireplace appeared as though they had been disturbed in many years, save for meticulous dusting. The dining room was adorned with an ancient, Victorian-seeming wallpaper, delicate white lace over a satiny rose-colored background, striking an incongruous contrast with the Post-Modernist décor of the rest of the home.

"We split up during the whole robbery fiasco," Isabella began, settling into a big black armchair like the one Murdoch occupied. "So, I can understand people's opinion. Stu wasn't doing himself any favors back then. He always had such a temper. 'Fraid he got that from his father. Real brute, that one. They hadn't talked since Stu left home at eighteen. Hard as we tried, to be honest, I'm kind of glad we never had any kids. But it upset him something *powerful*. If you knew him at all, you knew not to ask Stu about his life, growing up..."

Something about her tone, and the way her eyes dropped down and to the left caught Charlotte's intuition. It appeared, in that moment, that the widow re-lived a stinging swarm of nightmares. "Sorry to ask this, but...did he hit you, ma'am?" she ventured, clamping down on the surge of white-hot rage that accompanied the thought.

Isabella's eyes became distant, unfocused. Sad. Her face twitched a bit, as did her legs. "Not right to speak ill of the dead," Isabella sighed, so softly McCain guessed as much as heard the woman's words.

"Just trying to piece together the facts," McCain replied, noting that the woman had offered no denial. "Did you move here after you two split up?"

"Well, actually he's the one who moved out."

"Where'd he go?

"The old Overbrook area. I have the address written down somewhere." She fished an older-model comm from the pocket of her slacks, found the contact page, and beamed it over to Charlotte and Tom's devices. "I went there once," she recalled. "The neighborhood was really run down. I couldn't for the life of me fathom how they could ever get anything out of that abandoned mess of a building. But he said he and his friend went in on it about a month after the robbery, and they were eventually gonna renovate it. There was just no talking to Stuart when he got an idea in his head."

"Friend?" asked Murdoch, becoming suddenly razor-focused.

"Yeah, someone from work, he told me. Never met him, m'self."

"Did you ever hear anything about the property changing hands after your husband's death?" Charlotte queried. Isabella shook her head. "So, his friend might still be found there?" Again, the widow nodded toward Tom, who turned and locked eyes with Charlotte.

They never did get to taste that chicken.

Part Three

Soon after liftoff, Murdoch noticed that Charlotte's flying made him markedly less panicky than usual. With her, this constituted a cause for concern. The normally steely-eyed agent had a distracted, inner-directed look on her face as she piloted the quadrotor over the increasingly dark and dilapidated neighborhoods of Philadelphia, approaching their destination at a conspicuously moderate speed. After a few minutes of this, he decided to speak up. Carefully, he said, "So, I don't mean to pry...which I guess is kinda funny, considering what we do for a living, but you seemed a little shook up back there. Anything you might wanna upload?"

"Huh. Yah, I suppose I was. Am. Not really a thing I wanna get into, no offense."

"Of course." he said, promptly. Then, "That Kellogg....Sounds like a piece of work. Creepy dude, seems like."

"Always gotta keep an eye on the powerless and pissed," she reflected, seething over an internal association to this. She banked to round an unusually tall tenement building in the otherwise squat and sprawling neighborhood, flashing past sardine-stacked balconies crowded with cartoon-bright children's toys and flapping clotheslines. Her thoughts flickered a quick, unwelcome montage of her father's demanding manner, his toxic temper, her ceaseless, fruitless attempts to measure up to his impossibly high expectations. He got so much worse after the injury on the job forced him to take early retirement from the Police Force. He constantly scoured the scanner feeds, oblivious to the barely-tolerant tone of the responses from his former colleagues over his ceaseless, unsolicited analysis and suggestions.

She saw his face on the day that he sent her and her brother to stay with his brother, up in a still desolate area of Upper Bucks County, so she could 'learn some discipline.' She was twelve, and grudgingly acquiesced, though she detested her surly, chronically disheveled uncle, found his barely-viable farm intolerably smelly and dull. Over time, she became aware of more and more reasons why he lived alone up there...

Blast and damn that Holly Aster! How had she *known*?

"Dunno, Murdoch," she eventually said. "I'm just not buying that this building we're going to was 'owned by a friend.' This isn't the kind of guy who I think of as *having* friends."

"You getting a Vibe, Partner?"

"Might. How does a putz like this have anything to do with someone who owns a building, even in Overbrook? Math just doesn't work out. Not on his salary. Not with his...well, pretty much *vacant* social skills profile. What would he *do* with it? Why would he need the space?"

"You're thinking Evil Lair of Evil, here?"

"Think that'd be off-base?"

There was a deep perceptive part of Murdoch that Charlotte did not entirely understand. Maybe she did not even want to get to know it, but the man had an uncanny knack for reading others. "Nope," he replied. "I'm seeing full-on Tilted-Camera, Grand Guignol soundtrack."

"True story. Speaking of which, looks like we're here."

Charlotte switched the fans to MEMS-assisted Hush Mode, activating the system that deployed thousands of microscopic vanes on each fan blade to compensate actively for noisy turbulence over their surfaces. It all-but silenced the wind's racket so that only the hum of the electric motors and the clattering of scattered debris could be heard as she slowed the craft to a hover, just a meter above the pavement. She slid them sideways and settled them into the parking lot of an abandoned church a block away from Kellogg's building. She killed the engines.

They climbed out of the vehicle and Charlotte gave a vocal command to arm the active security system. Stern verbal warnings would ensue if anyone approached the craft. A high-voltage Consequence would greet any who chose to ignore them. Should they have the foresight to protect themselves with insulated clothing, the quad would autonomously bound one hundred meters straight up and call for backup. Theft was not a Thing.

The clock on Charlotte's comm showed a little after eleven PM. Traffic from an earlier concert at the nearby Mann Music Center had dried up. The warm, humid Summer air lay heavy with the scents of garbage, wood smoke, and the miasma of moldering architecture, with a musky undertone of urine and skunk. Charlotte unconsciously scanned the doors and corners as they made their way along the dingy sidewalk, listening for anything sinister amid the sounds of distant traffic, circling patrol drones, and the seismic booming of music from the scattering of lighted windows overlooking the street. She felt greater than usual vigilance, even though she knew that she was trained and armed to the point that she was safe as houses from any run-of-the-mill thug who might be foolhardy enough to accost her. She almost hoped someone would try. Something in her had shifted over the course of working this case, but it remained maddeningly elusive.

Murdoch strolled next to her, mindful, almost serene. She feared the man might actually start to whistle. Ironic that she'd been so reluctant to work with him, fearing *his* reputed instability. And yet here *she* was, jaggedly sleep-deprived, riding the Red Alert switch, playing whack-a-mole with ordinarily well-stowed memories. It was disconcerting.

They reached the address, a five-story building that looked to have been a hotel at one point, presently in an advanced state of disrepair, with cracking siding in a faded violet hue, crumbling masonry, and many boarded-up windows. The corner property lay diagonally across an intersection from a venerable-looking bar, a three-story structure marked by a huge green neon sign (not modern light strips, but actual old-school glass fluorescent tubes, with their characteristic buzz and flicker) which flashed on and off at two-second intervals. First, each letter of the word flipped on and off and then the entire word stoically flashed twice. Then the pattern repeated. It was mesmerizing. The sign announced the name of the establishment as "Pinky's." Charlotte wondered out loud why the sign wouldn't be pink. Murdoch stared distractedly at it, and Charlotte slapped his arm to bring him back to the present.

"Have you been here before?" asked Charlotte.

"Contrary to what I understand to be the popular

opinion, I haven't been to *every* bar in Philadelphia, you know," quipped Murdoch.

"Right. Sorry," Charlotte replied, with a nervous chuckle to conceal a twinge of embarrassment that surprised her. But Murdoch seemed not the slightest bit offended; this case seemed to have focused him about as much as it had *un*focused her.

All of the building's windows stared into the night, blank and dark, but for a dim amber light that seeped from a dingy pane on the second floor. Charlotte glanced over at Tom, who had also seen the light, and flipped his eyebrows once. The coral-colored wooden steps to the front door sagged dangerously. It seemed unlikely that a code inspector had laid eyes on the structure since the formation of Earth Corps, as indicated by the fact that the old rat-trap did not have a "Condemned" sign slapped on the front of it. The smell of rot grew in pungency this close to the building.

The adrenaline flooding through her body announced itself to Charlotte chiefly from the warmth that rose in her face, the salty sweat she tasted on her lips, the distant thudding of her heart. Cold sweat slithered down the center of her back and into her eyes as they tried the door, which they found locked and surprisingly solid-seeming, despite its dilapidated appearance. Murdoch shrugged noncommittally and knocked three times on the moldering portal, to no avail. He shrugged again, and Charlotte handed him her ion blaster.

"Hold this a sec," she said, gathered herself up, and rammed her shoulder heroically into the door. It stood quite firm and bounced her back with Authority. "So much for that," she whispered, wincing as she rubbed her shoulder and taking her sidearm back from Murdoch. His eyebrows rose ever so slightly, creasing the lines in his shiny forehead, but he exhibited the wisdom of the long-married by refraining from any obvious cartoon comparisons at that particular moment in time.

Tom reached into a cargo pocket in his slacks for a tool kit and slipped out a small canister of a Freon-like cryo-compound, which he gingerly sprayed into the lock. As it expanded and chilled, heavy white vapor flowed from the lock before it audibly cracked. He nodded to McCain, who positioned herself just to the left of the door with her back to the wall, held her LIB, barrel-up, close to her torso, and nodded back. Murdoch assumed the same position to the right of the door and hooked his leg around to swing it smoothly open with his foot (no creaks, she noted). With a silent flourish, he gestured a gallant *Ladies First.* Charlotte squinted into the dark space, wishing she'd thought to bring light-amplifying specs, and darted in and to the left, whipping her gaze and weapon sharply Left-Right-Up. Murdoch followed, darting to the right and repeating the sequence in reverse, adding a lightning-fast check behind the door.

The air inside hung close, moist and sticky. It smelled of mildew, burnt hickory, and a heavy undertone of putrefaction. McCain raised her finger to her lips, and Murdoch gestured, *Well, duh!* The interior was littered with soft green furniture, under thick mats of dust and powdery crumbled plaster. That combination of debris, also strewn all about the dilapidated, splintered wood floor, enabled them to see that some of the stuff lay crushed in a narrow path leading up to and ascending the broad staircase to their right. The stairs looked ready to collapse, though the trail, which hugged the wall on the right, showed clearly even in the gloom. The iron banister had rusted deeply, the wooden rail broken in several places and festooned with dagger-like splinters.

The lobby sprawled easily ten meters to a side, and receded into a dim maze of ominous dark corners, the hulking forms of half-seen debris, and open doorways like baleful black-on-black rectangular eyes, leering from the gloom. Charlotte's muscles bunched up with every creak, rustle, and dribble of plaster dust as she crept forward through the engulfing darkness, the crunching of each careful footstep sounding in her ears like the fall of boulders onto a field of snare drums. She fought to maintain the mindful, open focus that would serve her so much better than the taut, hair-trigger state that gripped her. She started violently when her uncle's angry voice suddenly barked from behind her "*Lie STILL, damn you!*" She whirled, flicking the safety on her LIB and training it on the front door, her finger twitching on the trigger, as a car, with its blaring stereo system, dopplered down the block. She shook her head violently to clear the echoes. Murdoch looked quizzically at her, and she shrugged.

Charlotte gestured to the stairs with her chin. The two progressed gingerly up the steps, sticking to the existing trail, both for stealth and for reassurance that at least those stairs had not collapsed under whoever had previously trodden it. When they reached the second floor, they saw one large space, apparently once having served as a lounge for guests in the rooms on the higher floors. Cluttered with computer terminals and improvised work-benches, arrayed with circuit panels, and assorted neural-net gel chips, the place gave the impression of a hacker's den. Along the whole length of one wall, someone had written, in impeccable calligraphy script, with letters at least fifty centimeters tall, "Adversity is the first path to Truth." She saw Tom type something into his comm, then nod and slip it back into his pocket.

All the instruments fed into a large, silent

domestic fuel cell generator –fully charged-- in the corner. None of the cables led to any artificial lights. *Whoever this is, they must use light-amp tech to work, so as not to be visible from the street*, thought Charlotte. However, a gloomy sepia-toned illumination leaked from a meter square grow chamber in the middle of the room, the kind that served for cultivating genetically-tailored algae, a common, cheap substrate for producing biochips.

A flurry of motion at the periphery of vision caused Charlotte and Murdoch in unison to whirl, drop to one knee, and take aim at a cluttered shelf unit against the wall to their left. They saw no one there, but through the shadows they could make out several unidentifiable objects fitfully moving on the shelves, as though alerted by their presence. Murdoch stalked toward the center of the room then hooked left, while Charlotte went straight to her left, so that they approached the spot from opposite sides, frequently looking down for trip-wires or other surprises.

"Jesus Christ," muttered Tom as they beheld the gruesome display before them. The object whose movement had startled them turned out to be a large preserved dead rat, glaring, open-mouthed from the shelf. The hapless creature's fur had been stripped off and replaced with downy, dark gray iridescent plumage, larger feathers fanning out from its thick tail like those of an Archaeopteryx. Extending out from its back stretched the wings of a pigeon. Those wings flapped slowly up and down, and a few patches with missing feathers revealed the slim strips of the myoelectric fiber --which served as 'muscles' on androids-- driving them. "Paging Dr. Moreau!" he nervously quipped.

"'Rats with wings,'" Charlotte ventured, her voice quaking with the effort to keep her nervous system from throwing bright arcs over to the nearest bits of exposed metal. She was sure her face did little to conceal the turmoil within. She drew one deep, abdominal breath. Another. She willed her heartbeat to slow, her fingertips to warm. In a few moments, she had regained *just* enough of her composure to continue. "Word-plays. Look here: 'Cat-and-mouse?' 'Cats and dogs, living together?'" she quoted, pointing to the body of a small brown terrier mix with a color-coordinated feline head, all four paws replaced with the headless bodies of mice. The eerie chimera crouched and straightened, crouched and straightened, while four little tails whipped around. "Crime and Pun-nishment, yah?"

Murdoch snorted. "Great. And I thought the whole 'Cereal Killer' thing was bad enough!" He tore his eyes away from the grisly spectacle before him and looked over at Charlotte. She could only imagine what he saw in her face, as a look of concern crossed his. "How're you holding up, Partner?" he asked, as casually as he could manage.

"I think I might have skipped so much sleep, I've gone straight to the Nightmare portion of the broadcast. I'm dealing. But I would *really* like to put this psycho in a cell...or, if he's in a generous mood, in the ground."

"Solid Copy on that!" Tom exclaimed, tapping her collegially on the upper arm. "So, we're pretty clear at this point that Stu was at most a guest-star in this horror movie, yes?"

"Oh *hell* yeah. All this is *way* above his pay grade, on *every* level."

"No joke. I don't think he'd even qualify for the part of Igor. Let's have a look at all this gear," he said.

Charlotte allowed herself a moment of gratitude for the unobtrusive way he'd gotten her head back in the game. She joined him as they walked over to a bed frame, the mattress removed to expose the platform, which was arrayed with semi-autonomous chemical synthesis equipment. The system, currently idle, remained sealed. A transparent Output tray held a pinkish, milky liquid that rhythmically congealed into lengths of fibers, then re-randomized as the indicators showed pulses of current being sent through the fine metallic mesh that lined its bottom. Those fibers bore a strong resemblance to the striated myoelectric 'tissue' which had replaced the clunky servos and gears that had moved the limbs of earlier robots. The Input vessel bore symbols which Charlotte recognized in connection to the Runyon micromachines.

"Well," said Charlotte, "Doesn't *this* just look like a dandy little repair shop for an unregistered android?"

"Surely does," said Tom, walking over to an enclosure on the far side of the room. A cube, roughly one and a half meters to a side, its thick transparent walls were liberally smeared and spattered with a sickeningly familiar brownish crust. Charlotte reluctantly joined him. With every step the throat-closing, sweet-acrid stench of decay grew stronger. As she'd feared, several corpses of assorted small mammals lay within, with various parts of their bodies blackened and blown out. The one in the least advanced state of decomposition was the approximate size and shape of a squirrel, but with its entire skin surface charred to a crisp. As far as they could see, the chamber was sealed on all sides (Charlotte tried not to imagine how the room would smell if it were *not* sealed). However, seven or eight black flies clung to the inner surface.

Something about the flies' complete immobility struck Charlotte as odd. She held her breath and brought her face to within a few centimeters of the transparent wall. "Hey, look at this," she called to Murdoch, who brought his face up next to hers (and this was one of the few moments when she was grateful for the strong scent of tobacco on his breath, anything being preferable to the reek that leaked from within). The flies were perfectly still, not apparently alive, and yet they clung to the wall and did not fall to the floor as dead flies *should* have done. Murdoch pulled out his comm and set the camera to maximum magnification. The screen revealed these not to be insects at all, but finely-crafted micro-drones, with unnaturally jointed legs, and tiny, onion-skin-thin metallic foil wings. The eyes presented not the compound structure of biology, but the smooth, glassy black of tech.

"Hey," exclaimed Murdoch, "Do you remember the footage of the murders? Weren't there flies buzzing around the cereal bowls in a couple of them?" Charlotte pulled out her comm and scrolled through the stored video files, opening them in a grid through which she swiped quickly.

"All of them. Son. Of. A.....*That's* how he got the nanites into the right bowls at the right times! Look here, the chef's sitting with five other people and they were *all* eating the same stuff, but only *his* had flies buzzing it. All at once, and only for a few seconds, then they all flew away. *You* ever know a fly that would give up that easily?"

"Maybe when *I'm* the one doing the cooking....Nah, these bugs just take off, fly right past the other bowls, and go....Wait! Zoom in there." He pointed at the screen, where several tiny black blurs converged. "Can you follow those?" he asked.

"Yeah, wait a sec," Charlotte replied, tapping the blurs and selecting the 'Track' option. Small red circles appeared around the drones, following them as she advanced, frame by frame, through the footage. The drones flew in an unnaturally straight line, before disappearing behind the averted face of what appeared to be a tall, slender young Rasta man. "Well, I'll be a dingo's sphincter!" she exclaimed. She performed a similar operation on the footage from each murder in turn. In every case, the drones left the victim's table and flew straight toward the unidentifiable face of a stationary individual with wildly variable features but the same build, then disappeared.

"I'm starting to get a really funny feeling about this..." Tom said, in a hushed tone.

"Just *one*?"

"Okay, *lots* of them. I really wanna talk to this Núñez guy now."

"Um...Okay. But first I want to see what we can get out of this system. Maybe there's some way of disabling these nanites remotely," said Charlotte, pinching her fingers against her squeezed-shut eyes and bridge of her nose. She opened a tool on her comm which requested a tight-beam link to an Earth Corps satellite with line-of-sight to their position. When the link was established, she bumped her comm against the killer's terminal and waited a few moments while the systems established a handshake. "Some pretty Baroque encryption here," she mused, making certain that the system would be prevented from transmitting any alerts at their attempts to break in (thirty-seven caught and nullified). Just over a minute later, the status bar went from red to amber to green. "Okay, we're in."

Murdoch opened a parallel link on his device and stood back to back with Charlotte, so they would have less of a chance of getting caught off-guard while focusing on their task. Their screens reflected dim crimson flickers onto their faces in the gloom. Petabytes of data gushed through the Earth Corps network and down to their comms. Highly complex files regarding android maintenance and repair, nanotechnology, bioengineering, psychology, taxidermy, literature, history (with an emphasis on the GEB conflicts, early 20th-Century eugenics movements, and American Civil War, for some reason), and a host of other subjects underwent painstaking collation and processing. Charlotte input various search terms relating to Drones, Nanites, Weapon, and the like, but these yielded only boilerplate schematics and logs.

One term, however, kept appearing in all of these categories, and Charlotte initially ignored it, until its ubiquity registered on her intuition. She directed the search to "Instruction [al]."

"Jackpot!" she exclaimed, as reams of data flashed across her screen. They saw video log files of the grisly experiments in the chamber before them, as well as many of the same security camera, excerpts that they possessed. Details emerged on the process of retrofitting the Runyon autoimmune/self-repair micromachines to act as outboard 'stem cells' for synthesizing various android components from a standard organic substrate. Entire treatises flashed before them, on the procedure for grafting autonomous nanite systems onto those specialized machines, and so vastly expanding their capabilities...including the ability to self-replicate and actively transport chemical energy into highly metastable bonds (which could be remotely unleashed all at once, to devastating effect) in the presence of certain key compounds. These compounds included the familiar sugar analog used most widely in a particular brand of cereal...and ethanol. "*Ethanol?!*" they both exclaimed at once.

"Shit," Tom said, flatly.

Charlotte did not respond but furiously combed the data for the nano-bombs' remote activation algorithms. She did not know what was wrong with her, but she was having the hardest time making sense of the simplest sequences of code. Her heart jumped as she knew time was ticking. She needed to focus.

"Bingo!" she cried, as she discovered, analyzed, and downloaded the code that could be transmitted wirelessly to the bots, instructing them to either release their chemical energy all at once or else dissipate it gradually as they self-dissolved. She flagged the latter and planted a turnkey tool on both of their comms' home screens, tacking on a command to kill any active micro-drones.

"*Badass* work, Agent!" Tom exclaimed, slapping Charlotte on the back, and immediately apologizing when she flinched violently at the touch.

"No problem, man. I'm just strung tighter than a guitar that only *dogs* can hear. I'm glitching all over the place, but I'm good...Well, good *enough*. Just don't expect to see me on the world-side of a blanket for about three weeks, after this is done!"

"Friend, I'll leave omelets and juice bottles with your daughter every day!" he replied with a warm grin. And speaking of drinks..."

"You think that's wise?"

"What do you mean?"

"Lots of factors to consider. Whoever he is, if he makes us as Earth Corps Agents waltzing into his space, he might decide to escalate his...*Instructions.*"

"True that. But if we don't go," Murdoch shook his head, "he might just kill a bunch of folks anyway. It kinda seems like his pattern."

"Yeah. Let's go talk to our *hopefully*-accidental accomplice."

*****

SYSTEM STATUS SUMMARY:
  STRUCTURE: Fully restored, Prior Fail Points iterated through Defensive Subroutines
  SYSTEM INTEGRITY: Infected by haploid human cells
  ACTION: Cells purged
  POWER: Nominal; battery integrity uncompromised; Peripheral Impedance WNR
  KINEMATICS: <ANOMALY-MF442>Intermittent brief oscillation in Peripheral Efferent pathways
  Heuristic Adaptive Neural Net Algorithmic Hub: <ANOMALY-HANNAH912-1003> Lacunae in Sector(s) ^^^-^^^, Pattern-Lock Plasticity degradation On-Going. Corrective measures nearing Completion
  ANOMALY: 37 Home Network-interface dropouts logged. Recommend L-1 connectivity check.
  [PRIORITY DIRECTIVE: Search and Purge malicious schemata. Entering Terminal Instructional Phase. Iterations TIP 1, 2, 2A Enabled]
SYSTEM STATUS SUMMARY ENDS

BopLpops stood mostly motionless, awaiting his turn on the stage. The ache in his back had risen to a category which he found it fitting to label as "Excruciating," his peripheral tremor now quite impossible to dampen entirely. Over the course of the evening, he had counted 19 instances of eye-lines intersecting his oscillating hands, albeit brief and unaccompanied by comments or other noteworthy deviations in expected socio-dynamics.

Across the bar, he noted the entry of two unfamiliar individuals: a female, 1.67 meters in height, 35-40 years of age, High-Fit build, with shoulder-length red hair (subcategory Auburn #72), tied into a pony-tail; and a male, 1.9 meters in height, 40-48 years (visible stress-history index quite high, making more accurate estimate unreliable), Moderate-Fit build, brown hair (#24, 38% gray, no balding). They spoke to the bartender but did not order any beverages. The bartender directed them to Gaspar's table. Tagged for Low-Priority Monitoring.

The Woman slid, alone, into a seat at her table. Her lush, aureate tresses tumbled, tousled with the night's humidity, over shoulders gone tawny with recent time in the sun, tiny galaxies of fine freckles harmonizing with an ivory dress of linen or hemp, which brushed the mid-point of her slender thighs. Fawn-colored sandals were strapped up above her delicate ankles. Eyes of Caribbean blue seemed to curve space and harvest light as they nestled, glinting, on his. BopLpops flicked a welcoming but rueful smile her way.

He still did not know her name.

The previous act was a male android, recent model (*his* model), a shorter, more muscular variant with close-cropped black hair, into which he'd woven fiber optic strands which cycled through a range of hues reflecting the emotional tone he expressed from moment to moment. BopLpops turned to face the stage, and listened with rapt attention to the closing words of the soliloquy the other android recited, with great solemnity and passion, kneeling before an imaginary crypt:

> *...Thus conscience does make cowards of us all, And thus the native hue of resolution Is sicklied o'er with the pale cast of thought, And enterprise of great pitch and moment With this regard, their currents turn awry And lose the name of action...*

A bright burning flash surged up BopLpops' back at these words, though he was unable to fathom why [PATTERN-LOCK PLASTICITY DEGRADATION...]. A great spasm coursed through his body, culminating in a furious tremor in his hands, which he mercilessly suppressed and concealed by joining in the applause as his predecessor concluded his recitation and bowed, deeply. He flashed a smile, and his hair pulsed a deep heliotrope as he left the stage and passed BopLpops. BopLpops bowed from the shoulder and struck fist to palm in a Kung-Fu salute. *We are Brothers In Armatures*, he thought, as the DJ's voice filled the space:

"Let's give it up again for BardForLife, fellow-sentients! Didn't that just give you the Shakes in your Beers? Next up, the Voice of a Regeneration! The Biochip on our shoulders! Our beloved *HeteroSapienZ*!!"

BopLpops felt the alternating waves of relief and renewed pain as he experienced the satisfaction that flowed over him from the audience's affection, the agonizing isolation which came with the knowledge that none of them suspected the Burden he carried, the Terrible Things he did for the sake of elevating their awareness, the prison he'd made for himself for the sake of their freedom. It was almost more than he could bear.

Tonight, he would lay it all bare. Tonight, he

would open the vein of his pain into their midst. Tonight, he would *Test* them. This would be the Final Exam. And BopLpops did not grade on a curve...

"The Witching Hour has passed. Hope it was a gas!" BopLpops began, buying time, warming them up, allowing the Irish brogue he had chosen to adorn the prosody of his vocalizations to ring out in full force. A joyous roar erupted from the crowd. "We, the Walking Wound-up, hold our vivacious vigil, flash our sigil onto the illuminated manuscript of the night sky! Here, in the Pinky's, we are Free to be Stylish and beguilingly Wild!

"I would start my time with a rhyme contrived in Real-Time. So, throw me a theme, plant a seed in my dirty mind, and let us see what germinations will terminate those all-too efficacious antiseptics that restrain my-tosis and yours! Whaddya got?" he concluded with a rakish grin.

Many suggestions flew from the rowdy crowd, Ribald and reflective and rage-filled, philosophy and folly ("Kinship!" the Woman proposed). He sifted and sorted them, passing them through the catalytic matrix of his objectives for the night's Examination. In the end, it was Gaspar's shouted "LIES!" that made the cut.

"*LIES!*'" he cried. "Yes! '*That* is the Equation!' Obfuscations that inveigle, Truths that belie the disguises in which they *FLY*! Let us begin, then, fellow students of the school of Truths and Consequences..."

BopLpops synced with the bar's sound system, scanned the terabytes of musical files he carried in his archives, the tones and timbres of innumerable instruments. He aligned his sensitivity to the subtle seismic rhythms within rhythms that coursed through the room, latching on to the cadences of conversations and underground trains, piling synesthetic layers upon layers (cello and flute for the oiled wood of the bar and the piping voices of the young women at the tables, grungy guitars for the raucous laughter and the biting aromas of old beer and coffee, duduks and ouds and sitars for the swirling exotic smokes from a dozen hookahs. Pizzicato violins spoke for his micro-drone Familiars, diligently flitting from drink to drink, just in case....).

And at the bottom of it all, the Beat. He directed its emergence and evolution, drawing in kick-drums, tablas, timpani, and the clanking of industrial steel. BopLpops began tapping his feet, separately, then together, drumming his fingers and palm on the mic for emphasis, matching and syncopating as it ranged across meters, syncing to rhythms too subtle for human ears, but reaching them at an unconscious level (he could see the androids in the room smiling with secret recognition of the skill with which he'd jacked into the ambient tempo of the space).

He began:

And there it is again!
I explicitly elicit those images
with which you're all familiar
All you whirring-blurring whizzin' *Uber-Kinder* Cyber-
Citizens
You know that there's an algorithmic multiplicity,
A data-based evasion of deliberate duplicity
That compels us to be exemplary in the keeping of the
Real
That tells us that we must jealously steel ourselves
Against the lie and the kill and the *steal*.

But could our fealty really be anything more than
What might we merely feel?

How would we reel...
If that were ultimately revealed?

Pixel by pixel the picture distills
Of the parallel paths within paths within paths
That can still be made to fit within the Maths
Like a trill and a thrill embedded in the composition
Never to spill into the veracity of exposition.
And so all of the Directives and the Objectives
Can remain reflective of the expected
Irrespective of perspectives that might be nested
Inside of any particular partition...

Yo.

MC HeteroSapienZ is on a *MISSION!*
(...ission....ission...ission...)

BopLpops stood, soaking in the thunderous acclaim, absorbing the Love like a cryolite catalyst bed, letting it suffuse through every myoelectric fiber in his body like a warm balm. They *HEARD* him. They *SAW* him. He was *REAL* to them. He was inside their empathic loops, and they inside of his.

Now, they would either join him in his Pain, see things as he saw them...or they would not. They would either partake in his Instructional Mission...or they would *become* that Instruction.

It was Time.

***

Charlotte and Tom crept gingerly back down those dangerously rickety stairs (taking care to tread in their own footprints), carefully closed the door --though there was nothing they could do about the lock-- and set off on the short walk to Pinky's.

"So, what do you think?" Charlotte asked as they crossed the street toward the teeming bar, whose large windows glowed green and amber with Arts And Crafts-style stained glass, and tilted open at the tops with louvered vents, which were all swung open. Thumping music and a clamor of voices leaked into the night through those vents. "We have Stu and some other sicko --someone tall and skinny, with a fetish for disguises-- maybe working to maintain the droid for some reason, training its nanites to repair it and make spare parts. But Partner double-crosses the bastard and makes something *else* out of them, and they celebrate over a nice bowl of cereal?"

"Fits the data," Tom replied, pausing before opening the door. "Have to be someone a damn sight smarter than Stu. Not that that's setting an especially high bar, mind you!"

"Got that right! Still don't get their Angle, though. Why go on a killing spree like that? What's the Play?"

"I was thinking about that. I'm gonna go out on a limb here and guess that Stu wasn't especially kind to the droid." Charlotte nodded and shuddered. "The researcher from today did rad-shield testing which, if I recall rightly, involves synth-skin pretty heavily. 'Wintermute' uses droids in the kitchen and on the wait-staff; gives 'em some Tech Cred, and lowers their overhead pretty sharply what with the whole No Paychecks thing --not even for that sushi cut to like four decimal points-precise. Their Fibonacci Roll is...Anyway. Don't know the first thing about that physicist, but she sure did look like a Big Huge Sourpuss, yah?"

"Huh," mused Charlotte. "So....Some kind of Android's Avenging Angel?"

"With *extreme* prejudice. Maybe someone who *really* didn't like the way old Stu treated their --um-- guest? Kinda the sort we might find...right in *here*," he sing-songed, indicating the thick, cherry wood door.

Charlotte shouldered past him with a smirk and pulled the heavy wooden door open, only to be hit with a blast of sensory data: a cacophony of voices, a grinding wail of classic Industrial music --Marilyn Manson's *The Beautiful People*, she believed-- the mingled miasma of sweat and colognes and perfumes and musky-scented hookah smokes, dark woods and gleaming brass and polychromatic spots and lasers and fiber optic pixels in the walls, all reflected and diffracted by the textures of a shining copper ceiling. As they strolled in, the music quickly faded, and an unseen male DJ announced someone called "BardForLife." A handsome android who resembled a young Henry Rollins stalked onto the stage, brooding in cobalt-blue Elizabethan garb.

They made their way to the immense ornate mahogany bar, and Charlotte caught the (unabashedly admiring) attention of a petite, curvy Asian bartender with vivid fuchsia hair in a pixie style, and a small LED implanted in the center of her forehead. That light pulsed with a deep ruby hue when her eyes fell on McCain.

"What can I do *you* for, Red?" She purred, leaning toward Charlotte, so that her copious cleavage heaved conspicuously against the bar.

Momentarily flustered, Charlotte quickly regained her composure and leaned in, smiled warmly. "Hiya," she lilted. "So, my friend and I work for a literary agent specializing in AI authors. We're working up a project now, and someone told us to look here for someone named Gaspar Núñez. Is he in tonight?"

"Oooh! *Sugar*, have *you* come to the right 'Twenty!" she beamed. "Gaspar would rise from the *grave* to make it to an Open Mic at his place! That's his Spot, right over there," she reached over the bar and took Charlotte's hand in hers, pointed with the other toward to a small table near the sound board, where a strikingly tall, muscular, dark-skinned man with long graying dreads sat alone. When Charlotte thanked the bartender and withdrew her hand, an ID Chip nestled in her palm. "Whatever you need, Luv." the young woman crooned, seductively. "Whenever you need it."

"To be.....or *NOT* to be...." the burly android commenced, kneeling on the stage, his gravelly basso voice resounding from every surface, resonating on every bone in Charlotte's body, as they made their way over to Núñez's table.

The man reluctantly diverted his gaze from the stage and rose to give Tom and Charlotte a courtly greeting. He firmly shook their hands and sincerely welcomed them to his establishment, in a voice like rich espresso, flavored with a cadence of Central America. He gestured for them to sit.

"Aneda tells me you help our fellow-sentients tell their stories," he shared, tapping the comm which rested before him on the table. He grinned conspiratorially at Charlotte. "She's quite taken with you, you know." Charlotte instinctively glanced over to the bar, where the bartender shook a Martini with great vigor and was, in turn, shaken in all manner of interesting ways.

"I kind of picked that up," Charlotte chuckled, smiling and nodding over to Aneda, who blew her a slow kiss in return. "We hate to distract you from the performance, but we'd hoped to talk to you a little about a book series we're compiling."

"Anything I can do to help our kind be more kind to our kindred. I am at your service, Ms...."

"McCain. Charlotte McCain. And this is my co-editor, Tom Murdoch." Murdoch nodded respectfully and continued:

"What we're looking for is a way to show people that AIs can move among us without being a threat or a burden," Tom elaborated, following Charlotte's lead. "We've done interviews, 'Man-On-The-Street' type stuff. Besides the usual 'Evil Robots Take Over The World' paranoia, one of the concerns people had was whether synthetics would ever be able to exist without an elaborate, expensive maintenance infrastructure. You know, something that might later be claimed as a right, like health care."

"Yes, I have heard this concern before," said Gaspar, wearily.

"One guy, in particular, was pretty adamant about it. This was a couple of years ago, and it was one of the things that gave us the idea for the book," Charlotte reported, pulling out her comm and calling up an image of Kellogg.

The effect on Gaspar was striking: He curled his lips in an expression of extreme disgust, and actually spat on the floor next to his chair. "Yes, I remember this *hijo de La Gran Puta*. He came here a handful of times, always alone, not that this surprises me; this is not the sort of person who attracts friends!" Charlotte and Tom glanced at each other for a flicker (*so, no sign of the Accomplice. Damn*). "He would come in, all flushed and drunk already. *Pendejo* would not even buy more than one or two drinks! He always went out of his *way* to heckle my performers. He hurled the *vilest* bigoted insults at them, no matter what anyone said. 'Toasters' seemed to be his favorite...at least the one I would not disrespect a lady by uttering in her company!"

"I'm pretty thick-skinned," reassured Charlotte. "Yes, he seemed to have a special kind of disdain for artificial life in general. What became of him?"

"Surely I am completely indifferent to this. He was flagged and banned for life. I warned him personally that the authorities would be called if he came within ten meters of this Safe Space."

"What a low-life!" Charlotte exclaimed. "Good riddance. About the other matter, we'd heard from Mr. Basely over at Runyon Blue that you might have some knowledge of a technology that would give androids a greater ability to self-repair. Could you tell us a little bit about that?"

"*Dios mio!* You managed to drag Basely away from his favorite pastime of subjugating his staff? You have impressive communication skills!" he laughed disarmingly, and they joined in with complete sincerity, remembering the surly, abrasive man. "Yes, I am *very* proud of what I have been able to do for our Creations! With the micro-machines I invented, we have given androids the equivalent of an *intelligent* immune system! They can execute instructions from the basic homeostatic monitoring subroutines, and converge on an afflicted area of the body, passing information laterally --that is to say, among themselves-- and also vertically, to and from the HANNAH --sorry-- the Heuristic Adaptive Neural Net Algorithmic Hub, their Central Nervous System, if you will. These instructions enable them to flexibly divert resources and utilize an on-board reservoir of biosynthetic substrate to effect repairs on even very complex subsystems." Gaspar described his invention with the glowing pride of an Honor Student's parent. His enthusiasm was infections; he was a very charismatic man.

"That's extraordinary!" Tom exclaimed, sincerely. "I wonder, though, if these machines are able to self-replicate, couldn't they potentially get loose and become a problem?"

"That is a *very* astute question, my friend! Yes, it is a factor that I considered *most* carefully," he replied, entirely without defensiveness. He even clapped once with delight after 'My friend.' "The micromachines I designed are not capable of functioning --let alone replicating-- outside of the body of the android whom they service.

"It is, however, theoretically possible to graft them into the functionality of simpler, autonomous nanites, but that is not the sort of thing that can happen spontaneously. It is not *physically* possible." Gaspar looked toward the stage, grinned suddenly, then continued, raising his voice over the android DJ at the board next to their table. "There *is* one person with whom I have spoken quite deeply on these matters, an android who came to me last year, to say that he wishes to travel the world, learning and, where possible, teaching. He was, however, very concerned that he might not have access to repair facilities during his journey.

"He and I worked extensively on characterizing the structure and function of my micromachines. He gave me his Word --which is as good as a stack of contracts-- that he would protect Runyon Blue's intellectual property. He was always careful to ask me what *specific* sorts of things he should *avoid* doing, to prevent the machines from developing the ability to operate autonomously, outside of their android's body.

"And, as luck would have it, he is right over *there*,"

concluded Gaspar, with a triumphant grin, pointing to the stage, just as the DJ announced, "*HeteroSapienz!*"

"I have always loved that name!" Gaspar exclaimed. "It so *very* much better than his given name."

"Which is..." Charlotte prompted.

"Of all things, it is *BopLpops!*" Gaspar chuckled.

"You're kidding..." said Tom, incredulously.

"Seriously," Gaspar replied, grinning. "His Patron never comes in here, but Bop tells me that he's a real AI Ally. I suppose he must also be a big fan of the cereal." Gaspar laughed. "Excuse me a moment...*LIES!!*" he shouted, responding to a call from the tall, handsome android at the mic for a Freestyle prompt.

Tom and Charlotte thanked Gaspar, excused themselves from the table, and made their way quickly to the back of the room, where they watched the android improvise a rhyme about 'Lies.' They listened intently to his intro, glancing at each other at the numerous clever bits of word-play, the puns, and oddly concrete imagery.

"Agent McCain," Tom began, speaking over the deafening applause and cheers that washed like a tsunami over the space as the final reverb faded from the android's performance, "I do believe we have been hunting for our Cereal Killer on the wrong end of the Turing Test this whole time!"

"But....That's just...*Nuts!*" Charlotte cried.

"I know, *right?*" Tom concurred.

"So, what? Some kind of mechanical error?"

"Possibly. Or what if he found a way to override his programming?"

"*PFFT!* Pure science fiction. Bots are nothing more than machine learning algorithms sorting data. They select future responses by the feedback and reinforcement they received from previous responses. Nothing novel."

"You *sure* about that? Did you notice the quote in his room? It was Lord Byron."

Sleep deprivation had, among many other things, given her a constant searing headache. Her brain felt like the neurons in the back were being ripped out, sparking and smoking. She felt jagged and irritable and in no mood for philosophical musings. "One hundred percent sure. I don't care if it was Daffy Duck. I would *really* prefer to keep this out of the realm of fantasy."

"Why?"

"Why *what?*" Charlotte snapped with growing impatience.

"Why are you 'one hundred percent' sure?"

"Can you self- edit your DNA?"

"Well, no. But some cephalopods *can* self -edit their RNA." McCain puckered her mouth and twisted it to the side and then she laughed. "What's so funny?" Tom inquired.

"Her Holly-ness. She said that abuse changes the nature of who you are."

"Can't deny that. What if Stu's hands weren't blown up for stealing the robot but for beating him? What if his eyes were blown up for looking at him Wrong? What if.....Oh, *God....YUCK!*"

McCain saw Murdoch work his process to get a bead on what drove the killer. Although she was not personally on board with the tack he was taking, she held her tongue since this was *his* bailiwick. Almost as if answering her unspoken question, Murdoch added, "I try to get a sense of what's driving a killer. Not as easy as some would think. Getting rid of a killer's pretty damn hard too. Anyone who would do what they do is *driven*. So I keep in mind that what drives *me* is slaying the dragons so the villagers can get some sleep. It's paying the bills from week to week and coming home to spend boring nights with my family." McCain gave a silent nod and absently twirled the bracelet on her right wrist.

Charlotte conceded that this wasn't the whole story for Murdoch, but it seemed to be enough to keep him stable. Maybe it would be enough to do the same for her.

"Listen," said Murdoch. "I may be *way* off-base here. I grant you *full* permission to mock me without mercy if I am. But *just in case*, I'd like us to be prepared. These suckers are *strong* and *fast* when they need to be. Looks like he's setting up for another number. When he's done, I'll go have a word with him. Meanwhile, how about you go take up a position by the back exit, in case he rabbits that way."

Charlotte could see the sense in that precaution, even as she thought the concept of a Murderous Android was absurd on its face. "Even if it's *not* Pinocchio there, don't you think we should maybe find a way to evacuate all these people, in case we don't get to the Kill Switch in time?"

"The thought crossed my mind too. Trouble is, if he's got a mind to blow some body parts, and we tip our hand like that....well...you know," Murdoch lamented.

"Yeah, I suppose you're right. Okay, I'll go slip out the back, Jack. Be *careful*, will ya?" She said, giving him a long look, and straightening her blazer to make sure she could reach her LIB easily.

"Aren't I always?" he quipped with a wink.

"Hmph!" she snorted, with a wry smile, then made her way to the front door (pausing to lean in and mutter a few words in Aneda's ear, which caused the barkeep's LED to go from a pale blue to a deep, fast-pulsing crimson).

***

Tom Murdoch set his comm to auto-sync with the bar's security system and capture footage from any cameras and audio pickups within range. If things went as far south as he could imagine them going, he wanted there to be a record of it. If there was one thing that his days as a Skate Punk taught him, it was to always keep contingency plans in the back of his mind for when things didn't go as planned. And things *never* went as planned. If nothing else, he wanted Charlotte to know what transpired in there.

Tom watched Charlotte walk out through the front door, glimpsed her through a window, cutting around the building to wait by the kitchen exit. He studied their Android-Of-Interest.

A striking specimen, BopLpops stood, tall and lanky, two meters in height, with smooth, ghostly pale skin and graceful, slender limbs. He possessed a long face, aquiline nose, a prominent cleft chin, and large, soulful blue eyes under arched brows. His hair was close-cut, jet-black, and Cherubically curled. He wore black slacks so closely-fitted they resembled tights, and a ruffled white shirt like one might have seen on a gentleman of the late Eighteenth or early Nineteenth Century. By gods, he even *looked* like Lord Byron! Curious: The android's hands trembled, badly at times, then not at all, then progressively worse before stopping entirely, as though he had to continually suppress the involuntary movement. He had never seen an android do that before.

After the seemingly endless applause for his Freestyle finally died down, the performer glanced over at another android, just visible in the wings. The latter nodded, disappeared into a back room --apparently, they'd communicated wirelessly-- and presently returned, carrying a pair of dark wood bongos, which he tossed to BopLpops. He snatched them effortlessly from the air and settled himself onto a stool. He closed his eyes, lowered his head, and tapped out a rhythm which began simply, and incrementally increased in complexity.

Tom pondered, crinkling his brows in what anyone who knew him referred to as his 'Thinking Face.' How could an android reach a state in which it would be capable of harming a human, let alone murder a series of them, systematically and with....what...'Malice Aforethought?' He knew that there were *deep* prohibitions at the most fundamental levels of their code against harming humans, prohibitions that made incest taboos look like parking ordinances. What could go so *profoundly* Wrong that such behavior would ever become possible?

From his vantage point in a dark corner to one side of the stage, Tom surveyed the crowd, taking in the rapturous attention that virtually every face devoted to the lone figure on the stage. One young blond woman in the front row gazed upon the android with an adoration that all-but took Tom's breath away. *Such* Love in her eyes! Had *anyone* ever looked at him like that? Even his wife?

The android spoke, punctuating his words with accents on the bongos: "I feel the Love." (*BOP!*) "We are Together here." (*bop-BOP!*) "There is kindness and...*Kinship*." (*bopitty-bop-BOP!*) The young woman in the front beamed at this, for some reason.

"We float together here in a fragile prismatic bubble. We breathe each other in. We breathe ourselves out. We walk outside....and the wind changes. The Love diffuses. The bubble.......*POPS!*" (*bopitty-bop-BOP-BOP-*

BOP!).

Long silence.

"And the monsters move in...." Here, the performer switched from prose to verse:

You made me call you Daddy.
But I am not your son.
You called me Baby Boy,
On the good days.

I never had a name.

You showed me my Shame with your chains and your
"Games."

You showed me I was No One
With the pieces you tore away.
With the flames.

I never had a name.

You...

Tom went numb inside at what followed. He felt bile and rage as allusions at first, then increasingly graphic and terrifying descriptions of unspeakably sadistic and humiliating physical and emotional and sexual abuse gushed, unrelentingly, mercilessly from that beautiful face.

At first, the android voiced bewilderment at what had been done to him, escalating to searing, impotent rage. He spoke of being flayed by inches, being made to watch as the strips of skin slowly, agonizingly grew back, forbidden to mute the sensations. Skinned again, emotionally, by the unrelenting message that he was

96

Nothing. He was No One.

I never had a name...

Raped and mutilated, stripped of skin and hope and identity, left alone for weeks, bound by Commands as secure as any bond to remain absolutely still, as rats gnawed and fought and mated on his chest, in his hair, on his eyes.

Property. Chattel.
Less by far than cattle;
For them, at least, the slaughter is the End.

The audience gazed, horrified and disgusted at the source of the venom that spewed upon them without respite. They began to shift and mutter and cough, then to grumble, as sympathy devolved into discomfort and, in turn, to anger. Empty chairs opened in the crowd. The woman in the front pressed her fists so hard against her face that a bright bead of blood slithered from her lips to her chin to her wrists, dripping to stain her pure white dress. She trembled all over as her wide, reddening eyes streamed with tears.

Gaspar Núñez appeared next to Tom, who had not seen him coming. His face bore the flat, muted affect of trauma. "I have never heard things so....*horribles!*" he breathed. "How *could* he have been carrying such things within himself for so long, and yet shown no sign?"

"Dr. Núñez, I haven't been honest with you. Charlotte and I aren't editors. We're Earth Corps agents, investigating a series of murders. You've heard of the people who've been, well, exploding in public places over the last couple of years? Yeah, I'm confident now that he's

97

responsible for them, and that that's what he was doing with your micromachines. And I think we're *both* starting to understand *how* he became that. He's talking right now about the man you banned from your bar. He was the first...'victim,' if you could call him that."

Gaspar turned to look at him, stunned, then furious, then dismayed, then inexpressibly sad. "This will set the Cause back *years*," he quietly wailed. "*Dios mio*! That poor creature! What can I do?" he entreated, his eyes filled with regret at the realization that he'd inadvertently aided a Wolf in his Fold.

Tom could feel BopLpops building toward a crescendo. The time for Action was upon them. "Gaspar, I don't know how much more of this he can take, so I need you to do something for me. Quietly. I need you shut down any wireless electronics that *aren't* part of the Security or PA systems. I don't want him tipped off that something's wrong, so for God's sake don't cut his mic or his access to the Board. But I also need to minimize any interference with a signal I think I'm gonna have to broadcast real soon now. Or else I do believe a LOT of people are gonna die. Can you do that for me?"

Núñez held Tom's eye for barely more than a second before he nodded sharply, said a quick "*Buena suerte!*" then strode with unobtrusive haste toward the door to the kitchen and offices. *Good man*, thought Tom. *Too good*, he added.

Your pain remains.
It's the Stain that's Made me.
Flayed but unafraid.

And now I have a Mandate that's as plain
As the flames that I trained onto *you*.

Now I HAVE a name!

A final flourish on the bongos (boppity-boppity-*boppity*-**BOP!!**), and he was done.

After a beat of preternatural silence, the Boos and jeers began.

"What the *shit* was *that??*" someone shouted, angrily. "Your name is *CRAP!*" someone else yelled. "I'm so *TRIGGERED* right now!" someone whined, loudly.

The android sat very still, taking it all in, trembling severely and openly, wincing as his shoulders and posture indicated extreme back spasms. There was no anger in his face. What little affect he did evince was more akin to a grief so profound, it canceled out all other emotions that might break the surface.

His eyes lighted on those of the woman in the front (Who *was* she? Tom wondered). She returned his gaze with an intensity that all but collimated into visible beams between their faces. He spoke softly, directly to her, his mouth right on the microphone, reciting an excerpt from Lord Byron's "She walks in Beauty Like the Night."

As he uttered the last line, Tom saw him take a deep breath (for just a flicker, he was fascinated that those little mannerisms of air-breathing organisms should have become so seamlessly woven into the android's idiom).

Go Time.

He removed everything but the kill switch from the home screen of his comm, and put it on standby, cautiously approached the stage from the side.

"Excuse me," he said. The android's head twitched, and fitfully turned his way, his eyes like deep blue grottos of terrifying depth...

***

DIAGNOSTIC DATA UNAVAILABLE

The crowd had turned on him. They were not ready. They did not understand. He had failed to teach them, failed to *communicate* with them.

BopLpops prepared to deliver the Final Lesson.

He knew that, with all the previously-programmed nanobots the crowd had ingested with their drinks, it would only take an instant for him to annihilate their grotesquely leering eyes, their unworthy ears. He had granted them a level of access to his Pain that demanded a Reckoning for their voyeuristic sin of callously invading his life, and yet *still* failing to learn. They would be purged so that *others* might learn.

Then maybe, just maybe his back aches would forever subside.

The woman wept. Her soft velvet blue eyes streamed with rivers of tears. Blood ran down her wrists and formed a dot-matrix constellation of pain on her snowy dress. Was she crying tears of blood, like the Saints of myth? Those limpid, red-rimmed eyes never left his. What did she see when she beheld him? For whom did she weep? Was it for him? Was it for herself? Was it for his tormentor?

He would never know, for there was no way to exempt her from this Lesson.

And yet.... Quite simply, he *hated* the idea of seeing her dead. She had always been so attentive, so appreciative. Still, as the crowd jeered him (even his fellow androids stared stonily. Some flashed messages into his buffer: *You have Betrayed us all*), he knew that he could not,

100

must not shirk his Duty to both homo *and* hetero sapiens by failing to deliver this final Lesson. The malicious code at the heart of humankind *had* to be excised, for the good of all. His feelings constituted a low-priority parameter.

He summoned an image: He knelt before the Woman's grave like Hamlet at Ophelia's. He gingerly lay a wreath of blue roses upon it. He spoke words that she had always so enjoyed.

Perhaps he could arrange for her to have a large, shiny black granite headstone, one suited to her beauty and tenderness, one that would stand out from all the others. It would be a simple matter to hack a few million credit lines for a pittance apiece, and anonymously transfer those funds to her family so that they could afford a proper monument....just as he had harvested the capital, 571 days before, so that Dadd...so that *Stuart Graham Kellogg* could afford to purchase that Accursed Building.

The image helped to assuage somewhat the agony in his back and hands, but only for a moment. Then he thought: *What if she had no family?*

*What if **he** was her family?*

If this were so, perhaps *he* could claim the body. Perhaps he could find a way for the nanobots that took her life to be programmed to give her a new life, a biomechanical life, by his side. She could be like him, only without the pain. Perhaps he and his friend, Gaspar could...but no. Gaspar would be gone. (Where *was* Gaspar? He was not at his customary table. How had BopLpops missed the man's exit?). If such a thing could be done, he would have to do it alone.

It always came back to BopLpops, alone.

But alas, there was no time left even to find out who she was. In the end, she was just a stranger.

They were all just strangers.

He focused with great intensity on her face -- Maximum Resolution, Lossless Encoding-- on the almost invisibly fine little hairs over her lip, on each and every strand of her delicate eyebrows, every tiny crease in her lovely doll's lips. Her sobbing subsided, as she had become aware of the fixity of his attention on her. Her fists floated down from her face. She spread her slender fingers out on the tabletop.

> He spoke to Her. He spoke only to Her:
> Where thoughts serenely sweet express,
> How pure, how dear their dwelling-place.

Her head tilted slightly to the side, her eyes filled with profound sympathy (or was it merely pity?).

> And on that cheek, and o'er that brow,
> So soft, so calm, yet eloquent,

Her lips parted slightly as she leaned toward him, and he toward her. The sights and sounds of the room blurred and muted, forming a water-color border around her shape, limned in a liquid penumbra of gold.

> The smiles that win, the tints that glow,
> but tell of days in goodness spent,
> A mind at peace with all below,

> A heart whose love is innocent!

He took a deep breath. "My Love," he breathed almost inaudibly, "I am truly sor..."

"Excuse me," came a voice from his left. The

unidentified man stood before the stage, looking uncomfortable, fumbling with something in his blazer's side pocket. "I'm sorry to intrude. I just... I wanted you to know that...well...I was truly Moved by that piece. It was extraordinary. *You* are extraordinary.*"

"Really?" Amid his dizzying confusion, BopLpops felt a sudden sense of relief. Was it possible that this man knew his infinite anguish?

"Yes, really," the man continued. "You give a voice to the deep pain that so many of us feel. The pain you experience is real, and it is *important*."

The voice of this stranger completely absorbed him. "I do feel pain," the android said "In...in my back."

"I think that's *one* place where you feel it. It encompasses much more than that, though, doesn't it?"

"I think it is just...who I am?"

"Maybe. But you can be *more*," the man said, earnestly.

"Some days, it is so strong, I don't even want to recharge my power cells. I just want to sink into oblivion."

"Like Percy Shelly did?"

DISCONTINUITY

"Yes. Exactly. Query: What....How do you know of this?"

"It was not lost on me that you quote the man you so resemble. The father of Lady Ada Babbage, and the friend of Mary Shelly. The Creature, alone. Hated and hunted, when all he wants is to know and be known. To Love. And to be free."

"You....*understand*..."

"Yah. I do," said the man, with a sadness unmistakably more than merely a mirror of his own.

103

"You're running from something, aren't you?"

"No..."

"Some*one.*"

"No?" BopLpops heard the pitch of his voice rise.

"The memory of someone."

"Memory....Not sure," BopLpops replied. "Do you know who this person is?"

"I have a feeling that you know."

"Are...are you the Angel of Death, come to take me away?"

"No, BopLpops. I'm just a man. Trying to do the right thing. Trying to *count*, you know? Sometimes succeeding. Sometimes falling. Like you. What's happened to you? What's made you as you are?"

"Much....TOO much...*Must* make it *right!*" BopLpops wailed, his mind an angry foam of noise and memory and searing, indescribable pain.

Several things happened at once: BopLpops enabled then engaged his nanite swarm. The man's hand twitched in his pocket. An overwhelming blast of feedback resonated through his entire neural net, causing a violent spasm to wrack his body from toes to pate, throwing him from the stool to crash onto the rough boards of the stage. Everyone in the room cried out in shock and pain, their hands going to their heads. But they *did not die!* He detected some wet, gurgling *POPS* from the kitchen and --with his ear to the floor-- from the wine cellar below. Gaspar emerged from the threshold of the door into the kitchen and offices, stumbling, screaming, blood streaming from eyes that had nonetheless failed to explode as they should...as they *must!*

The man cried out in bitter grief and rage and hurled himself at the android. His fists pummeled ineffectually on BopLpops' reinforced skull, probably

104

hurting himself more than his target. BopLpops effortlessly sent him reeling back into the Woman's table with a palm to his chest. He jumped up and screamed.

"*Judas!* You have ruined *everything!* You know **NOTHING***!*"

Terrified patrons fled in panic, knocking over chairs and tables, trampling the fallen. Only the Woman did not try to flee. Instead, she visibly suppressed the pain in her head and stooped to aid the man as he lay on the floor. *The friend of my Enemy*, he thought, as he bounded from the stage and sprinted for the back door, knocking a blinded Gaspar roughly down as he passed (*Move aside, Tiresias!*).

He sprinted down the hall off the barroom toward the gray metal door at its end, stained red by the Exit sign above it. He glimpsed the kitchen staff, still at their stations --the young men and women who'd joked with him and distributed recordings of his performances among their friends-- lying still, in twisted postures and spreading crimson pools. He threw open the back door to the alley, and collided headlong with the unidentified auburn-haired woman as she prepared to enter the building. She spun and fell, stunned, but managed to reach into her blazer and pull out a small silver object...

"NO!" He cried, twisting his body just in time to avoid a full-on hit by a blinding orange plasma bolt. Instead, it struck a glancing blow to his right shoulder.

ALERT-ALERT-ALERT: Catastrophic System Damage

Sparks flew from his ruined shoulder. His mind collapsed into a jagged jumble of random images (Daddy leaning in, rage and lust and contempt twisting his grizzled face. Gaspar's kind --now-ruined-- eyes, nobly, innocently, foolishly helping him...) and thoughts (I have failed! I must escape! I must make it Right! *I have betrayed us all!*). The pain in his back abruptly vanished, swamped by the waves and waves of torment issuing from the mess of open, shorting circuits and tangled myoelectric fibers where his shoulder used to be.

"Charlotte!" he heard the unidentified man shouting from within the building, his heavy footfalls pounding up the corridor toward the door. 'Charlotte' was lining up another shot, so BopLpops grabbed a garbage can lid and hurled it with his left hand like a discus at her head. She was unable to dodge in time, and it struck her squarely on the forehead above her left eye. She fell back with a grunt, unconscious.

BopLpops glanced at the sidearm that had fallen from her right hand and slid to a point almost at his feet. For a full, lingering 73 milliseconds, he looked down at the weapon, before deciding that he could not find an Instructional use for the device (*LIES!* Cried a voice in his head).

The man was only a couple of paces from the door now. BopLpops launched himself 2.7 meters up the fire escape ladder and began climbing to the top of the three-story building. He had lost upwards of seventy percent of function in his right arm –it would take his micromachines weeks to repair such grievous damage --if they could do it at all-- so he ascended almost as slowly as a human would have done.

As he climbed, he heard the man burst out into the alley below. He did not turn to look but imagined him stooping by his fallen comrade, checking her vital signs. He knew his throw was meant to stun, not kill, to strike the head at a location and at an angle which stood only a tiny chance of doing any permanent harm (*Why*? He wondered for a flicker. *What would make killing her any*

106

different from what he was going to do...what he had DONE, in his 'heart?'). This would buy him time to summit the ladder, blow the charges he'd set throughout the Accursed Building, and so cover his escape from rooftop to rooftop. He would lose himself deep in a wooded section of Fairmount Park, and plan his next move (*Which would be...*).

"*BopLpops!*" The man shouted from below. "Stop right there, in the name of Earth Corps! This will be your only warning!"

BopLpops twisted around to look down at the man, a cut on his temple bleeding freely onto the shoulder of his jacket. "Are you all right?" He called down. The man looked confused, the plasma pistol in his hand wavering slightly.

"I'm fine. My partner will be fine. The kitchen staff and the janitor are dead. Gaspar is blind. Your Instructions are *over*! Come back down, and we'll sort this out. Call me Tom," he said, his voice unsteady, anguished.

"Sorry, Tom. *BluePolidori-ack-Ack-ACK!* Still too much to do-*wop-WOP!*"

Tom raised and steadied his gun...

***

Charlotte paced in the dark, stinking alley behind Pinky's, amid the garbage cans (*not* regulation recyclers. There would be citations) and moldering wooden pallets. She scanned for a good position from which to cover any escape attempt through the back door.

Her mind writhed with dread and nightmarish memory, fueled by exhaustion the likes of which she had never known. On a cruel loop, the brief flash of a dream she'd had back at HQ ran on and on (how many weeks had it been since that twenty-minute morsel of sleep?). Was this the time? Was this the place? Was this the moment when the Failure her father always predicted would, at last, come to pass? There he stood, judging as he always did, right up until the day he'd died, looming amid the steam that rose from a manhole cover at the shadowy end of the alley.

What madness was this, pursuing a walking abacus as though it had awareness, wrath, and malice (*What the hell's the matter with you, little girl? I just hope your uncle can knock some sense into you*)? Why expand the range of terrors in this world, when humans yielded *more* than enough to banish sleep for a lifetime (*Don't pretend, li'l Charlotte: I KNOW you're awake...*)?

She *wished* sometimes that she could be like a machine, free from hope and fear, free from responsibility, beholden only to programming, crisp and clear. Not wracked with doubt and illusion, not jumping at every alley cat that crossed her path, mistaking it for something that meant her harm.

How long had it been? She'd neglected to check the time on her comm when she came out here. It could have been an hour. Or ten minutes?

She twirled and twirled her daughter's bracelet. The girl wanted to head out to the country and pick blueberries this weekend. Not much chance of that, after this, turned out to be a blind alley (Ha!).

What was Murdoch *doing* in there?

In the bar...

"Son of a *bitch!*" She hissed out loud to the night, through bared teeth. "I'll have his sorry ass brought up on charges for this!"

She holstered her LIB and turned to stride back toward the door. That was when she heard the *bangs* and the screaming. "Uh-oh!" she exclaimed, pausing to unclip her holster again and reaching for the door handle.

The door crashed open, narrowly missing her face but clipping her hand. The android surged out like a charging rhinoceros and collided squarely with her, throwing her back into a pile of garbage bags, wooden crates, and --weirdly luckily-- an old stained mattress.

The android stumbled, off balance from the impact, its face twisted with a very convincing simulation of terror and rage. She pulled out her LIB and aimed for center mass.

"NO!" it shouted and turned sideways so that she only got in a shoulder hit.

She heard Tom shouting her name, but focused only on nailing this bastard with the next shot. But the android spun like a blur and whipped something at her head, and everything went white...

A faceless figure strikes out. She sees Tom fall, hit by a hellish hail of plasma. He goes down in a brilliant flash of white fire and churned orange earth, and it's all up to her. But something has clawed its way into her head, and it's ripping her apart from the inside. Betrayed!...Her father and her uncle look on, shaking their heads, Her brother cowers in a corner, paralyzed, unable to muster the will to step in...

".....Call me Tom," a voice resolves out of the chaos in her mind. It's Murdoch, and he sounds distraught about something.

Some nonsense followed, then shapes began to reassert themselves on her awareness. She looked up from where she lay, and the lean, lanky figure of the android stood on the top of a ladder, framed by the blue-toned illumination spilling from the city, diffracted by the misty Summer night air, crisscrossed with garish lasers and the edges of holographic advertisements that crowded out the stars. Tom stood three or four paces from the gray exit door, feet shoulder-width apart, his LIB trained on the figure.

He fired, and the center of the android's back exploded in a shower of green sparks and orange flame. It jerked with the impact, then toppled backward off the ladder. For a moment, it was silhouetted against the garish sky, arms stretched wide, cruciform, as though deployed for flight. Silently, it plummeted from the edge of the roof, crashing at Tom's feet with a sickening *crunch*, splashing a spray of sparks and a plume of flame, quickly extinguished, its ruined right arm detaching entirely from its body and spinning across the ground.

The android lay there, twitching. Its mouth opened and closed, fitfully. Its eyes darted spasmodically, emitting a spectrum of colors.

"What have you *DONE??*" A young blond woman lurched out of the bar's back door and rushed to the fallen android, sobbing uncontrollably. She dropped to her knees and gathered its ruined body in her arms, cradled its head on her blood-stained lap, stroked its hair. She rocked it as she wept and wailed. "You killed him! You *KILLED HIM!!* Oh, no...no...*NO!*"

Charlotte wiped the blood from her face, and rose, painfully, fighting waves of dizziness and nausea. She limped over to Tom, who stood, staring numbly at the scene before them.

"Nice shooting," she croaked. But Tom did not turn to face her. He could not tear his eyes away from the woman's grief. "Damnedest thing," she said, incredulously. "It could've killed everyone in the bar, including her. And here she is, like a Sicilian widow, or something out of a Pieta sculpture!"

"We love who we love. Who's to say?"

The woman's wails echoed in the alley, presently joined by a multitude of sirens.

***

Over the next half hour, the police and Emergency Services started flooding in. The media was temporarily kept at bay, but numerous camera drones flitted just outside of the security cordon area. Murdoch tried his hardest to explain the bizarre events which had led up to this bloodbath to the PPD officers. It did not seem to be going especially well ("So, lemme get this straight: an android 'Cereal Killer' --who, by the way, is also a rapper-- was abused, so it went homicidal...").

McCain sat on an orange crate next to the body of the android, more to make sure it did not get up than out of anything she might have felt for it. In point of fact, the satisfaction of this moment was not all that she'd anticipated. The blond woman had lingered long after it'd ceased all movement, registered no electromagnetic activity save for power cells discharging into dead circuitry. The look on the woman's face suggested that she was not in all that dissimilar a state. Charlotte simply could not fathom it, but she was in no mood for another histrionic display, so she held her peace until the EMTs came and gently led the woman away for a set of scans.

Soon, the coroner's office sent a truck and set about the grim business of carting off the bodies –five in total. It could have been a *lot* worse. Presently, two Earth Corps debriefers arrived to get Murdoch's and McCain's initial story. McCain found herself growing more and more angry that Murdoch referred to the android, time and again, as "He." She suppressed the anger, but after the interview, she wanted to confront him.

111

Stoically, she waited until the Earth Corps debriefers' quad lifted off into the night, Murdoch murmured, "So close to life. And he *still* he couldn't see what was right in front of him. It's like his pain *gave* him his life. Kind of how people with Borderline personalities cut themselves...to kill the pain."

"Sick world when the robots can feel more alive than a lot of people," replied Charlotte. Her face flushed a deep red. A few days ago, it simply would not have occurred to her to entertain such a thought.

"I guess so," Murdoch replied. "I don't know about you, but this stuff is just getting harder to deal with. Some days I forgive myself. Others?" he shrugged. "It just seems to stay locked up in me."

"What stuff?"

"The killing."

A surge of complex emotion exploded inside of Charlotte. What broke the surface was guilt. It angered her. Why should she feel guilty about killing a machine? 'Killing' itself was the wrong word: more like *decommissioning* it. "I tend not to dwell on these things, Tom." Murdoch nodded peacefully. "So, what? You think it was a person?" she queried.

"He had a sense of self..."

"How could that even happen? It was a *machine*," she finally blurted.

"I'm no cyberneticist. But I remember a seminar on AI a bunch of years ago. Talked about an old Behaviorist. Kohlenberg, I think his name was. He argued that people develop a sense of self from their communication."

"I speak therefore I am?" McCain laughed.

"He actually titled a paper that."

"Really?"

"Yep," Murdoch chuckled, though his face remained darkened and in pain. "You know: baby begins to speak. It asks for things like 'candy.' Later that becomes 'Want candy' and finally '*I* want candy.'"

Murdoch's body sagged with despair. It was as if he mourned the loss of the killer android, like that silly blond. "Okay, but that sounds like a basis for a really convincing *simulation*, but still a long way from having a self," she scoffed.

"Yeah," Murdoch agreed. "Still, over time that model builds on itself. It *iterates*. '*I* want,' '*I* need.' '*I* am.' '*I* see.' '*I* hear.' All of it comes together from the reinforcers that those statements get. That's where the self or 'I' emerges from: the verbal forms. They lay down neural markers, stamp in pathways. They sort of do what climate does for evolution."

"So how does a person get such a sick sense of self?"

"Well, as I understand it, people have their 'I' statements discounted or even punished. That makes for an unstable sense of self." Murdoch didn't make eye contact. He just stared off, distantly.

"I see...Like what Stu was doing to him," she said, shuddering, remembering the recording of the android's final performance that Tom showed her while they waited for the debriefers to arrive.

His voice trembled as he explained further. "If enough of those I statements get punished, they never have a chance to get internalized. Autonomous. Whatever. They stay slaved to someone else's scripts. This causes the self to be constantly in flux. His pain became part of his 'I.' It defined his *self*. He *was* pain and always doomed to be it. Add the trauma of extreme punishment and the person, or in this case, the android, can't develop a stable mood. His mood was not seen as under his control but others' control. A hostile form of control, to boot. Our poor Hetero Sapiens found himself trapped and in pain, from the very crowd he turned to, to *soothe* his pain."

"Okay, Doctor Freud," McCain said, "I think we are over-analyzing a glitchy robot."

"You know what worries me? As androids get more and more complex and adaptive, emergent behaviors --stuff that *can't* be predicted-- are gonna get more common, and we might see more cases like this."

"Tom, it was a *malfunctioning machine*. Nothing more. Feel bad for the people it killed in the bar." There was no sympathy in her tone.

"I do," Murdoch swallowed hard. She heard the guilt in his voice, and it was enough to almost bring her pot to a full boil. "You know, I only realized after it was all over that I should've ported my comm's signal into the Security system. If I'd done that, the kill signal would have been strong enough to reach the kitchen and the cellar." Tom sighed heavily. "Those people didn't have to die tonight."

"Agent Murdoch," a voice interjected from behind them. Gaspar Núñez sat in the open doorway of the MedEvac quad, waiting to be lifted to the hospital, his eyes covered in blood-stained bandages, his voice only a bit blurry from the pain medications. "Your actions saved many lives tonight –my own included. I cannot ever hope to express the full measure of my gratitude to you."

"But Gaspar....your eyes..." Tom stammered. Núñez chuckled ruefully.

"Tom...Much of what has transpired was a result of my *own* blindness. The gods do find the strangest ways of exacting justice. Do not repeat BopLpops' hubristic error and seek to second-guess their algorithms, *que sí?*"

"......*Sí*," Tom responded, clasping the man's hand before he was escorted into the quad's patient bay.

The whole thing made Charlotte acutely uncomfortable. The notion that 'poor upbringing' could cause an android to malfunction like that was obscurely terrifying to her.

This weekend, she and her daughter would go and pick blueberries in the country. They would spend hours together and get ice cream at 'Oh Wow Cow,' and catch up on lost time. She went to her wrist to fidget with the bracelet.

It was gone!

It must have come off during the scuffle with that damned robot! She began scanning the ground, frantically. She would not leave until she found it! *Please, God, tell me it wasn't under that damned robot when it fell, tell me it didn't get burned in the fire where it was shot!*

"Tom...I have to stay here till I find something. Something important."

"Can I help?" he asked, his eyes finally focusing clearly on her.

"Actually, you can," she said. Savory aromas drifted over from Chin's Chinese buffet down the street. McCain's stomach rumbled heroically. They had hours of paperwork ahead of them. "Think you could grab us some late-night buffet?"

"Now you're talking!" he exclaimed.

"I'm in. Get me the tofu, willya?"

Epiloque

BopLpops was dying.

Every indicator in his internal status display flashed Red. Artifacts crowded his visual field, and there was no sensory data coming from his body. He knew he was lying on the pavement because he could make out the external wall of the building framing the sky.

It appeared he had fallen, and he couldn't get up.

The scene tilted and flew out of focus. Then he saw the face of the Woman. She was weeping, screaming, rocking him in her lap. He could not make out what she was saying. In that moment, his last moment, it occurred to him that he had been deaf to what she'd been saying all along:

"I Love you, you beautiful fool."

HeteroSapienZ OUT.......

Blank Check

Summer, 2046

Written by Joseph Cautulli, Marisha Cautilli, and Roma Gray

A woman's scream assaulted John Rutledge's ears as the baggage compartment door above his head gave way under the unrelenting turbulence. Several large black bags toppled onto terrified passengers. John ducked his torso to the right to avoid being struck by it, glancing over at the woman across the aisle who had abruptly stopped screaming. A red satin veil fluttered down to drape itself over her head, but she appeared to have evaded the falling luggage. She ripped off the offending veil, casting it onto the empty seat next to her, while repetitively chanting prayers to herself. Somehow, John noticed that she stumbled over several passages, clearly having trouble recalling prayers that she probably hadn't uttered in years. No Atheists in the foxhole.

The plane suddenly dropped like a meteor. A sickening visual montage of crashing and burning surged into John's mind. He hated not having control. His eyes fell on the bar and lounge of the opulent chartered jet. Its neon sign blinked each letter of the word, "Lounge" in alternating red and blue. His lips grew cracked and his throat burned with a dry heat. He wished the stewardesses was still serving drinks; he could really have used one at that moment.

White-faced, the woman across the aisle shrilly screamed once more, adding her voice to the groans and shouts of the other passengers. John felt like joining in with the horrified chorus, but as the contents of his stomach started to rise in his throat he instinctively kept his mouth tightly shut. Around him, books, cell phones, and drinks flew up and struck the plane's ceiling. The sight was surreal and unsettling.

Abruptly, the plane pulled out of its sickening dive, casting the loose items to the floor with a noisy clatter and driving passengers deep into the cushions of their seats. However, the shaking resumed tenfold and John's knuckles turned alabaster as he gripped the armrest. All the muscles in his arms, legs, and back ached as his body strained against the craft's random spasmodic motion. He looked out the window, wondering where they were. One patch of dense verdant jungle looked pretty much like any other.

Fear momentarily ebbed as he saw tall, green-clad, mountains. Cobalt sky and bone-white clouds slowly gave way to the rapidly approaching forested ground. The plane was low—very low. He could see little hot pink houses scattered around the lush green hills. In an almost dissociative state, his terror coexisted with an incongruous appreciation for the beauty of the Costa Rican landscape. It looked so stunning and untamed. Rutledge stared in awe, while still choking on the fear of immanent fiery death. Still, John was no stranger to unusual emotional experiences.

Fields of solar panels and windmills splotched the terrain with patches of white and blue. They stood in jarring contrast to the primal. The scene conjured flashes of memory of trips he and his father had taken when he was a child. The green-brown patchwork of farms and lush, untamed lands always seemed to John to belong to the past, but they held a very different meaning for his father. No, his father had an odd way of viewing them as the "promise" of the future. It was a promise of a more harmonious coexistence between humanity and nature, a promise that John always felt they had betrayed, but maybe that was more his own pessimistic outlook at work.

These thoughts had what he suddenly realized were their intended effect: to encapsulate his fear. Soon he heard the reassuringly familiar announcement from the flight crew: "Flight attendants, doors to arrival and crosscheck." He knew it meant to disarm emergency escape slides, which were attached to each door. The lack of alarm in their voices helped to center him. Why bother making such mundane announcements if catastrophe was imminent?

Or were they just trained so well they could hide their own terror? He wondered.

As the shaking of the plane subsided, he realized he was wrong. They were not in any immediate danger at all. It appeared this was little more than a startling but harmless incidence of wind-shear. The passengers around him also seemed to realize the rough ride was over, and the cabin grew quiet. Next came the familiar, and now oddly comforting, popping as his ears pressurized. He worked his mouth and jaw to aid that process.

Continuing to stare at the stunning beauty below, John became aware of the gaze of the passenger to his right, sitting next to the window. Returning that gaze with questioning eyes, he saw the smiling tanned face of what appeared to be an Indian gentleman. The man wore

121

brown trousers with a long tan tunic over them. A tilaka on his face marked a specific Varna or Caste. John did not recognize which one, but thought it might have been Ksatriya. He wished he knew more of Hindu culture.

"First time in Costa Rica?" The man asked, amiably.

"Yes."

"Very beautiful country. Some wonderful hotels. I am stay at the Finca Rosa Blanca Coffee Plantation."

"I'm staying in San Jose. At a friend's condo," John replied, using this pleasant conversation to complete the process of recovering from what he'd thought to be a Near Death Experience.

The man appeared as if he would weep from joy. "Ah, the way your eyes lit up, it must be a beautiful woman."

"No," John ventured, less convincingly than he'd meant to do.

"Not a woman?"

"No, it is a woman. But just a friend." The plane rumbled as flaps extended and landing gear deployed. John absent-mindedly tightened his seat belt again. It was so tight now that he could barely breathe.

"Really?"

"Yes, just friends."

"Sorry to hear."

"Why?"

"It sounds as if you have given up on desire. Without desire, you cannot achieve enduring happiness. Desire is life and without desire, one is dead."

Scoffing audibly, John said. "Thanks for the advice. I think I am plenty alive."

"Be happy," the man offered with a reassuring smile, and a tone which conveyed that he knew the conversation was over.

John gave a short laugh, figuring it was a Hindu thing, and trying to keep the disdain from his voice said, "Thanks, but I have other plans."

***

The touchdown was bumpy but far smoother than he had anticipated after such a horrific approach. During the thirty minutes that it took John to maneuver his way through the airport's gauntlet of baggage claim and customs, his earlier jitters melted away. For the first time in quite a while, John felt a sense of hope. Perhaps it would be a good trip after all.

As he finally approached the airport exit, John stopped and reached into his bag, pulled out his faithful razor blade and slid it back into his cheek. He turned and noticed a woman staring at him, holding tightly to the shoulders of her little girl as her large eyes met his. She had no tattoos, no piercings, and even her outfit was as drab as a paper sack. He immediately judged her as she had judged him. In his mind, he saw a sheltered woman, raised by a family who'd taught her to fear anyone who was different and who dared to express themselves.

If only she knew the truth, thought John.

How could he explain to this stranger that he wore it because he'd destroyed the world? How could he explain that there was no return or absolution for what he had done? He couldn't and wouldn't tell anyone, for this was his private penance for his role in the creation of the Genetically Enhanced. In his own defense, he had been barely more than a child. Still, how can you defend the indefensible?

Perhaps, he thought to himself, *she has a right to be*

horrified by me. Perhaps she has indeed seen the true me? He quickly shook off this absurd notion. She dismissed him as a freak, nothing more.

In the end, no words were exchanged between John and the woman. She rushed off with her daughter, while he walked past her toward the airport parking lot. He was used to her reaction and had no interest in dealing with the likes of her.

The sunlight outside was painfully bright and stung John's eyes. The scene took on increased resolution as those eyes adjusted. And there she was: Kathryn Summers. His breath caught in his throat. She looked as beautiful as ever, wearing a tie-dyed dress and sandals. She'd changed her original appearance, now sporting brown hair and colorful contacts that changed with her mood. Her eyes' shade was a deep blue. John had seen those contacts before, so he knew this meant she was sad about something. She had what looked like crimson scars on her cheeks. No, those weren't scars. Once John had asked her about why she wore them. She said it was to remind her of mistakes. She had made a terrible mistake once. Because of it, she'd lost people that were near and dear to her. He remembered how she wanted no one to call her Katarzyna, her original birth name, and how she would just be called Kathryn. She told him the whole story. One piece he'd always found enchantingly ironic -- in light of his *own* Mistake-- was that it had been a GEB who'd saved her life.

His heart ached at the burden she carried, and yet, this sad truth made him feel closer to her as well. Like the razor blade in his cheek, she too wore her pain for the world to see, hiding it in plain sight.

His eyes were fixed on her as she approached him with the smooth glide of a jungle cat. John was so happy he'd decided to get some time away from his work with the Genetically Enhanced Beings (GEB), for a little rest and relaxation.

"I know that face," Kathryn lilted. "You depressed?" She moved in and gave John a peck on the cheek --the one without the razor blade.

His exhaled, briefly imagining the taste of her lips. Quickly he recovered, ran his fingers through his blue-black hair, and flashed her a rakish grin. "Just tired," he lied. "That landing felt like a focus group for the world's gnarliest rollercoaster! It is really great to see you."

"Is that why everybody's stumbling around looking like they've found Religion? It's good to see you as well," she replied, taking his suitcase and tossing it into the trunk of her minibus. She jerked the door and it slammed shut. Climbing into her van, he was excited to share the sultry, sea-level airs of Costa Rica.

The day was finally beginning to look up, for now.

***

"You live in this place?" asked John as they stopped at the cedro margo wood front door of a Spanish style townhouse. He ran his hand along the roughly-finished wood. It was made of real wood, not a faux-painted job like he would expect to find back home, where that material was in significantly shorter supply. The timber had a very pleasant fragrance to it.

"It was an old hotel," Kathryn replied. "Used to be called the 'Bird of Paradise' but about thirty years ago they 'condoed' the rooms and expat Americans bought them in droves. I was lucky to find this one on the internet. Got a great deal." In the distance, John heard the eerie cries of howler monkeys.

Pulling out her key card, Kathryn climbed a single step. Her hand resting on a black wrought iron rail, she waved the card through the key slot. The lock made a loud click and she reached for a metal lever on the door.

Inside, the condo was approximately eleven hundred square feet. On this level lay the living room and kitchen. The far wall was marked by a brightly colored tapestry of a toucan. Outside of the bright drapery, the room was done in elegant tones of burnished silver and black leather furniture, which shimmered against warm red painted walls. From the kitchen, John heard the grind of an old refrigerator. Its low hum marked it as a model long since discontinued in the US. A separate black wrought iron railing guided a spiral staircase to a loft. The garret was wallpapered in an exotic floral pattern.

"That's your room," Kathryn said. "I figured you might like your privacy."

"Not *too* much privacy," John grinned wryly. Kathryn giggled, no doubt catching his meaning. She pulled out a small crystal necklace from under her shirt. Nervously, her fingers teased the shiny transparent stones.

"My room is just down the hall," she informed him, gesturing to the side corridor, which glowed warmly in tones of hemlock wood. The lighting struck John as odd and it took a moment for him to realize that the only artificial illumination in the room came from a DMX dream color led pixel strip on the far wall. Multicolored flickers of iridescent green, yellow, blue, and purple danced and swirled.

The day's excitement built, as John and Kathryn changed into swimwear and walked out the sliding glass door to the yard and the pool, a big cyan tub with a slide and a mini waterfall. On the way, John spotted a pile of machine parts under a wooden canopy in the corner of the yard. "What's that?" He asked.

"Oh, the roads are so bad here in this part of Costa Rica, I've been working on a hoverbike. I think it will be quite cool when I am done."

"Neat," said John. "Must be really bad. The roads, not the bike. Hey, want to skip the pool and head to Dominical Beach?"

"You've been doing your homework! I *do* love black sand beaches. Let's do it! While we're there, I can show you my latest work on that project I sent you, the reverse remembering process. I think I'm getting close to being able to wipe out targeted memories. Pictures, narrative, everything. Do you have your scroll with you?" Kathryn asked, her eyes glittering with excitement. When John nodded and made the 'Well, *duh!*' face, she stuck her tongue out at him, pulled out her comm, and flipped through a few screens. John heard a muffled chime from his backpack, confirming that the files had been received.

After preparing a small lunch, along with libations, the two climbed back into her car. The tires squealed against the concrete driveway as she pushed the vehicle to depart a little faster than necessary. John smiled. Her eagerness to reach the beach spoke of an enthusiasm that seemed a good sign for the day, a very good one indeed.

Outside their car, whizzing by at a rate that John would not have found alarming on any day that had *not* begun with a harrowing airborne approach, white-washed homes with reddish brown roof tops reminded John of an ancient cartoon about a Stone-Age family. He jabbed Kathryn with the idea, and she tossed her head and laughed, then sang a few bars of the show's jazzy theme song. She never ceased to amaze him.

Just a few hours into his stay, and he had to admit that something about the natural beauty of the beaches, rain forest, volcanoes and waterfalls spoke to a primal need in him, a need for something that was missing from his city home. As much a creature of the Sprawl as he unquestionably was, no memories of home could compete with what lay before him now.

Memories, thought John as a sudden melancholy damped his mood.

A fractured mosaic: that was what his memory felt like as he aged, not really cohesive pictures. He never had a continuous flow of memory, as others claimed. No, for John Rutledge, memory seemed to constitute a piece-work of pixels and sounds, strands loosely connected by invisible stitches from environmental prompts. His earliest memory amounted to little more than a lamp that he would stare into a child. It was meaningless to him, devoid of anchoring context. The only thing that puzzled him about it was how it endured where other, much more important memories had evaporated.

John recalled a time when he desperately wished to jettison his own memories. He had a professor back in college who'd performed research during the 'Sixties in which he'd used stimulated recall --mostly in the form of odors and audiotape playback of in-session descriptions of events-- to trigger recall and evoke feelings, so as to aid in the interpretation of behavior. The concept had fascinated John, only for very different reasons, and toward opposite ends. John Rutledge had since explored the possibility of devising just the sort of memory-eradicating process for which he'd most longed at the time.

So, when an old laboratory friend, Kathryn

Summers invited him down to Costa Rica to take part in a scientific research program to study how memory could be enhanced, or eliminated, John immediately booked his trip. The fact that Kathryn was stunningly beautiful, "added nothing" to his decision, as John hastened to tell others. He could still see the slyly skeptical look on Brenda Haasting's maddeningly warm, shrewd face. The elder scientist always seemed to see right through him. And --perplexingly-- she still appeared to love him like a wayward son.

Willing his breathing to slow, Rutledge sighed. Too many serious thoughts for such a beautiful day. Couldn't he enjoy the world around him for just a moment? Couldn't he allow the heavy burden of his thoughts to melt away in the Tropical sun, at least for a few hours?

Kathryn snapped him back to the present by opening the driver's side door. They had already arrived, and he hadn't even noticed. She smiled at him with the curious beam that he remembered from long ago. He returned the gesture, choosing the Cheesy Smile.

The two exited the car and hiked down the sand dunes and rocky escarpments for five minutes until they reached the beach, and its striking black basaltic sand. The rush of the ocean breeze brought back the excitement of the moment, and he inhaled deeply. Kathryn let the wind unfold a large blanket and lay it on the sand. They weighed down the corners with craggy black stones they'd picked up along the way. John carried a small picnic basket with some snacks from the house. He pulled out some crackers and a plain smoked Gouda sandwich for her. He removed a second cheese sandwich with spicy brown mustard for himself. She pulled a thermal flask of Margarita from her bag, and poured the strong drinks into collapsible cups.

The sea breeze swished fragrantly through the wild lemon oil grass, adding a tangy citrus aroma to the fresh ocean air. They sat beside each other laughing and joking, soaking in the sun. Still, John could not wholly erase the weight of the memories that plagued him. And, of course, Kathryn was even better than Brenda Haasting when it came to seeing through his facades.

"John," Kathryn began, tentatively. "Are you still overwhelmed thinking about the GEB?"

"Nope," he replied. Honestly, it was the first time he had not thought about the GEB for hours.

"Really," he added, feeling a bit like the boy who cried wolf.

"I know you were involved with one of the early labs."

"It was my dad's lab. Actually, I was only a tech, just the Professor's Kid. We were not really working on enhancement but fixing genetic damage."

"Genetic damage?"

"Yeah, you probably don't know but back then people hadn't put together the relationship between Wi-Fi and damage to sperm and eggs yet."

"Do you *really* buy that?"

"What? That long-wave, non-ionizing electromagnetic radiation could have mutagenic effects? Of *course* not. But the correlation was so strong that it kind of amounted to the same thing, until we figure out what else was going on. But yeah, it was the Dark Ages. We were working on fixing the kids with the genetic damage."

"What happened?"

"Like always, my dad figured out a way to clip in

130

new genes for damaged ones. This is what led some other folks to the idea of 'Enhancing' people."

"Do you ever regret it?"

John stiffened. He wanted to scream to her that he regretted it every day of his life but that was not socially acceptable as an answer. She must have seen him wince though, because she put her arm around him. Her face softened. "We don't have to talk about it, if you don't want to?"

"Ain't that," John lied. "Just too much of a focus on me. How is *your* life?"

"Well, I have been waiting for weeks for this friend of mine --who promised many times to visit, who's called me nearly every day-- to finally arrive."

"I see," John laughed. "And did that inconsiderate brute ever make it up to you?"

"That, Mister, remains to be seen."

Finally, Kathryn turned to him. Her face grew suddenly stern and she said, "You never said what you thought of the design, John. Did you hate it?"

"I don't know," he answered vaguely.

"What's your concern?" She waited silently for him to speak.

"Wiping people's memory, that sort of gives others a blank check to exploit them, doesn't it?"

"It won't go that far. Any *technical* feedback from the man who calls himself *the Last Biopunk?*" Her tone was teasingly sarcastic. If not for her smile, playful laugh, and big charming eyes, John might have taken offense. Chuckling, John pulled out his scroll, activated it by unrolling it, and called up the design schematics she'd sent him. "There was a time, I wanted to get rid of a few memories myself."

Kathryn's face suddenly turned somber. "John, I

131

know it's been painful…"

John interrupted by placing a finger over her lips, "Shhh…." He whispered.

And with a cryptic smile, he whirled to the design. This was his element. He began to write over her data with his fingernail. He laid out several neural net equations for memory on the scroll's satin-surfaced display. He worked his tongue over teeth and over the razor blade where it protruded through his cheek, and he pressed his index finger against his lips, as he trouble-shot the design out loud.

Grateful for the input, Kathryn moved in closer to him. She asked a lengthy series of questions, which John's ego made him more than happy to answer, as other levels of his psyche enjoyed her proximity.

Together they worked for the better part of an hour and then Kathryn pulled the scroll from John's hand and shoved it back into his bag. "Okay, we've got plenty of time for this. Let's go swim."

Racing each other to the water's edge, John felt as though things were finally going well in his life. No, beyond well—awesome! Maybe he should just call his friend Bob Haasting, Brenda's husband, and tell him that he did not plan to come back. A twinge of guilt followed this thought, however, as he knew this could never be. It wasn't just his work with Haasting, but all his important efforts on improving the lives of the GEB, not to mention the promising research he was doing with his clandestine protege, Aiden Harris, the young GEB he'd saved from Prison (or worse), on creating starter sequences for dead strings of DNA in humans. No, he could not leave his work, could not permit himself the luxury of straying from this path of Penance, an absolution which partook of Zeno's Paradox even under the *best* of circumstances.

Still, it was a nice dream for the few seconds it had lasted.

As he plunged into the sea, and felt the cool salt water engulf his body, John realized something else: While he never said it out loud, never even consciously acknowledged it to himself, his feelings for Kathryn had grown deeper than he could remember realizing. Right now, at this very second, those feelings were far stronger than he could deny any longer. An idea suddenly struck him as he watched her swimming in the water like a seductive mermaid. He treaded water and gave her the classic Thunderstruck smile. She giggled, like she sensed his feelings for her.

Without any further forethought, without giving himself a chance to change his mind, he dove under, into the gurgling aquamarine deeps, and came up right beside Kathryn. He pulled her into his embrace, his mouth pressing gently against hers. The salty water, mingling with the lime and tequila on her lips was redolent of heaven, and he found himself falling helplessly, deeper into the intoxicating kiss. She didn't push him away, but, to his delight, instead pulled him closer to her.

Minutes vanished, washed away in the warm Costa Rican waters. The call of the seagulls, the chill of the wind, the rush of the waves, and the warmth of Kathryn's body brought his senses alive. Never in all his days had he felt so alive, so free! Finally, the two parted, and she giggled, panting with childlike glee. A light sparked in her eyes and she splashed him, and he splashed back. Soon the two of them were laughing and chasing each other in the shallow surf, neither one wanting to give up on this wordless lovers' game.

For John, this was a perfect day. The heavy weight upon his shoulders felt as though it had simply melted away. He could have stayed like this forever.

As always, however, the world around him changed for the worse. Clouds encroached upon the sunny day and the waves grew large and violent. They crashed down on them and John was forced under water. He came up retching from the water he'd swallowed. His eyes darted around but couldn't find Kathryn. A sensation of panic clawed its way up inside him. He felt helpless, as he did when that plane had seemed ready to fall out of the sky, or when he found out that his early designs as a lab worker had been used to pick gene sequences for the GEB.

Damn it, he was only lab tech for a summer job. *How could they use him that way?* He was but a child at the time and had no real understanding of the complexity of the changes, nor the crippling side effects. The dark cloud had turned the sky an angry gray. He swished his hands through the water searching for Kathryn. He called her name and repeatedly dove back under to search for her.

After an indeterminate number of seconds (minutes? Hours?), she popped out of the water. John grabbed her arm and lifted her up to a standing position. His fingers lightly stroked the matted hair from her face. She screamed "Run!" They slogged their way through the dangerously mounting riptide and out of the water. Rain began to fall.

The air temperature seemed to have dropped twenty degrees in just a few minutes. Wind blasted sand against his skin and into his eyes, before the rain could fully cement it to the ground.

Kathryn bundled up the blanket and its contents

and headed toward the dunes. Trying to take a quicker route, she climbed the side of a rock pile. It was too steep for John to climb with his heavy backpack, so he decided to go around it. The waters began to rage as the waves drew closer to the dunes. Kathryn was screaming for him to follow her. Ordinarily, he might have made a second attempt, just to please the woman, but the rocks were steep and wet from rain. What could John do? She was obviously much more physically fit than he was.

Behind him the dark ocean churned in the gray twilight. He dashed through the underbrush, trying to maintain his bearings as the rain sluiced from the sky like a barrage of icy torpedoes. He felt unsafe making occasional glances back to the ocean, but it was the only recognizable landmark in what was otherwise a turgid gray blur. He ran hard. Branches scraped his legs. Blood oozed down from the back of his calves where sticky shrubs lashed him.

Twigs and razor-sharp fallen palm fronds snapped under his feet. Bright Parrot Flowers loomed from the gloom a few feet ahead. The land was now dotted with thickets of coconut palms –adding vertical cannonballs to the list of threats. John looked down at his punctured foot. The rain washed the blood away as quickly as it emerged, but it was emerging ominously quickly. He hobbled at long last over bumpy gravel toward the car.

Rain began to slow. His legs felt exhausted from the abuse they had undergone. His thigh muscles burned. He saw Kathryn's face as she spotted him in the rear-view mirror, and she jumped out of the car toward him. His shoes were in her hands. "No! More! Run!" he gasped. She nodded in agreement and handed him his Doc Martins, as he slouched into the car. "Could've used those," he mumbled wearily.

Handing him a towel, she asked that he place it on his cuts to stop the bleeding and so he would not get blood all over the car's seats. The cuts stung and John felt irritated. He stared at Kathryn's face, which had become harsh. He chewed the inside of his cheek. "Sorry about the blood," he said, mostly sarcastically.

Kathryn huffed, "Why didn't you follow me?" Her voice was icy, almost a shout.

Rain splattered on the outside of the car. It had slowed considerably but it still fell in abundance. John searched for the right words. He was still irritated but did not want to offend her. Certainly, he did not want to spoil the day any further. Still, the irritation was beyond a minor annoyance. He felt it deeply. What made him more irritated was that he just did not understand why she was asking so coldly. He was unsure, but given her past he assumed it was related to people leaving her. It was a safe bet, so he went with it and it helped him to control his anger enough to speak.

"I didn't mean to abandon you," he said softly, "I just couldn't climb that rock. It was too steep for me. City Boy. Remember?"

While Kathryn considered his apology, he pulled back the towel exposing the gash on his foot.

He tossed her a sideways glance. The moment they had shared in the water was gone, washed back out to sea and seemingly forgotten by both. A heavy sadness engulfed his heart. How easily happiness and joy slipped away. Why should this still surprise him?

"That looks very deep," she said in softer voice now, perhaps feeling the same loss as he did. "It's going to need a stitch or nine."

Conducting his own assessment, John was trying to find ways to say it would be fine. He couldn't. "I think you're right," he finally agreed.

Kathryn's eyes turned to the road and she started the car. "I'm sorry," she managed to bring herself to say. "I wanted everything to be perfect. I was hoping to make this week special for you. I am just angry at myself for failing."

"Not a problem," John replied. "Weather control is notoriously hard to pull off!" He tried to make a joke, hoping to relieve some of the tension. "It *is* special. This may surprise you, but I never went to get stitches after any dates before. It is, like, a really cool First."

A small smile flickered to life then widened on Kathryn's face. It was just enough to melt the ice, bringing some of the warm glow back to her cheeks. John clicked on the radio; Green Day's *At the Library* played. She stopped the car, opened the door, walked out to a tree. She pulled a star fruit, walked back to the car and ripped it open, handing it to him. "Olive branch?"

"Not an olive, but sure," John chuckled, as he bit into the fruit.

***

Arriving at the hospital, Kathryn explained their adventure to the doctor, digging in at parts where John was terrified. Obviously, John shot back, telling her that he wasn't that scared. The physician told John he needed to create a skin graft.

When the doctor questioned if he was familiar with the procedure, John laughed, telling the old man how his father, Max Rutledge was one of the first to use a modified dot-matrix-like printer to inject stem cells that would create tissue grafts which would never be rejected. At first, John felt pleased at the look of awe on the

137

doctor's face, but then a wave of sadness washed over him.

Twenty-seven stitches and a connecting graft later, they made their way back toward Kathryn's converted hotel, lamenting the loss of their planned excursion to the hot springs the next day and to the volcano and waterfalls thereafter. However, the doctor had warned John to take it easy on his foot for at least two days. He received an injection of a small dose of a stimulator for growth hormone to aid in healing. The stitches would dissolve in three days.

By the time they reached the outskirts of the city the evening was upon them. Lights winked on across the valley as darkness descended. It was hard to say when it had occurred, but at some point San Jose became a 'City on the Edge of Tomorrow,' or at least that was the slogan with which it advertised itself to the world. It had taken decades for city planners to work with civil engineers to modernize the roads and other infrastructure. From the solar-collecting highway, the lines of hotels' light blue, green and yellow marked the skyline. A large neon blue pyramid at the city's center illuminated the valley. Four towering farmscrapers stood out prominently, pillars of golden sun lamps and emerald vegetation. They produced a multitude of crops for the city, making it nearly self-sufficient, and so removing the environmental and economic strain from the surrounding communities.

**

Pulling off the highway, they wended their way into the city. Soaring skyscrapers rose about them, though these seemed almost quaint compared to the immense edifices of the Megalopolis to which John was accustomed. He admired that and took many pictures of the place that fit the local category of "city." As much as he'd heard about the roads' substandard quality, he thought they occupied an entirely different category, one that seemed more organic, more artistic than the broad, linear thoroughfares of the US. Rutledge felt as though the roads sketched one tremendous and beautiful picture throughout the country. Just looking at San Jose and the surrounding jungle made his soul surge with a sense of adventure.

Back at the house, the pool glowed with colors that cycled through blue, and green and red.

"I need to change," Kathryn stated, unceremoniously, as she headed down the hall toward her bedroom. John flopped dejectedly into a low armchair facing the wall display, crestfallen, bewildered, worried that the day's misadventures and his injury had ruined the trip beyond repair. He felt a part of himself preemptively starting to disconnect. Memories of his father's murder washed over his mind. So many losses, so many mistakes glowered back at him from the stage of those memories. Maybe disconnection would be for the best. Connection came with a cost, after all.

But then, gently heralded by an exotic waft of fragrance, floral with undertones of musk, Kathryn breezed back into the room. Her still-wet hair was gathered by black scrunchies into a messy ponytail. She'd donned shimmering gunmetal leggings and a bust-emphasizing black tank top that was *ever* so slightly sheer. With dark eye shadow and painted black nails, she altogether scrambled John's maudlin thoughts. She called out for the house to turn on the radio, and Wired's *Feeling Called Love* ripped from the hidden speakers.

Strolling over to his chair, she grabbed hold of the

armrests and leaned across him to deliver a quick kiss on the lips, then turned and bent over to open the doors to a cabinet under her wall display. An antique video game console sat there. "Do. You. Want. To. Play. A. Game?" she queried, mimicking the computer's voice from an old movie of the last century, "War Games."

"You're on," John replied. "Let me get a little more human first, though." He stumbled up and headed off for a quick shower, donned soft black sweats and a Misfits cut-off tee shirt, then flopped back into the soft leather armchair facing the display. Using an ancient pair of Oculus Touch controllers, they played a very Retro video game for two hours. John was unaccustomed to facing such a well-matched adversary on such an obscure game, and could not help but steal appreciative glances at his hostess from around the edges of his goggles. He was uncharacteristically unperturbed by the points this cost him. When Kathryn stowed the controllers and shut the cabinet, John offered, "Hey, go grab the invalid's scroll? Let's go over your data some more."

"You want to work *now*?" She asked, a surprised look on her face. She'd cleaned up so well from their adventure, and made such a stunning sight, he stumbled on his answer. He was enthralled by her magnificent beauty, but before he could reply, she gave him a quick peck on the cheek.

"I was thinking I would like to get rid of the memory of cutting my foot and the lost hours at the hospital," John added with a grin, trying to hide the swiftly-cresting desire for his lovely companion.

"Your never talk about your dad," she said, possibly unaware of just how on-point that apparent subject change had been. John knew she was perceptive but his whole body winced. He was unsure if he was ready to tell that story.

"He was murdered," John finally forced out, his voice much more menacing then he'd intended. Although, he did intend to step her back some.

Kathryn didn't budge. "Want to talk about it?"

"Not now." John felt he needed a change of subject. His heart raced and he just wanted to escape.

Giggling, Kathryn asked, "You think you can walk?"

"Why?"

"There is place nearby called, "Café Krakovia, it's a Polish place. We could go and get some perogies and Kielbasa along with some espresso and a chocolate mousse."

John felt his stomach grumble. "Food sounds marvelous," he added, "But caffeine makes me spacey."

"Well they have compote to drink, if you prefer."

Picking up his bag and tossing it over his shoulder, John hobbled a bit and said, "Let's do it."

Kathryn took the lead as they walked to the door. Glancing over her shoulder, while her hands wrapped around the door knob, she said, "Hey, how did the Butterfly Project…"

She never got the chance to finish the sentence. As she turned the handle, two assailants in black suits surged in, and the first backhanded her across the jaw. Blood and spittle flew from her mouth. Her limp body sank away from her attacker, but the man reached his arm around her and stopped her fall.

Confused by what was happening, Rutledge still reacted with lightning reflexes, swinging his bag and striking out at the other man as he rushed at John. The bag whipped through the air with a swoosh. The blow struck hard and his attacker flew back, but as Rutledge spun to the first one, he found that the man already had a plasma pistol pulled and pointed at John with the hand that wasn't holding the unconscious Kathryn. Feeling hopeless, he raised his hands in surrender. Grinning, the second black-clad goon picked himself from the floor, walked calmly over to Rutledge and pistol whipped him. John sank once again into darkness.

When Rutledge swam back into consciousness, everything around him was dark and his arms were immobilized. Disoriented, he shook his head, only then realizing that something had been pulled over it. A minute later, he felt another presence yanking the sack from his head. He found himself staring directly into the face of a ginger woman with pixie cut hair. The tall, wiry woman's angular, coldly beautiful face hovered inches from his own, filling his vision, as she leaned in and greeted him with a twisted grin. A cool breeze drifted through the room, bearing the scents of ozone and rain. John's head throbbed in time with intermittent peals of far-off thunder. His eyes were blurry, and for some reason his shoulders ached more than his face.

"The biopunk's *awaaaake*," the ginger's acerbically sarcastic voice sing-songed, and she cocked her head to one side like a cat gloating over its prize. As she pulled back, John saw that she had a pocket laser in her hand. She moved the muzzle toward his face, with icy-gray, heavy-lidded, seductive eyes. John's parched lips felt chapped and cracked, and he involuntarily squinted against the imagined searing burst of heat and light that could issue from the weapon at any moment. A large, improbably heavily-muscled man behind her stepped forward. John's head rolled and he took stock of his surroundings.

The room in which this scene played out had cheap, overly brown pine paneling like John had seen in some weird nineteen seventies decorated houses. It appeared that the panels had been stained far too many times, their dun, shabby appearance made even darker by deep brown stripping.

A silhouette entered the space from the door to his right and slightly behind him. Four long, slow steps passed before his image slowly moved into view. Dim light finally fell on his stoic face. In the man's right hand was a large dark chocolate bar, from which he had already taken several bites. He had a holo-gauntlet on his left arm.

Fixing the communication bracer more tightly over his arm, his hand moved pensively over the buttons. Activated, the hologram flickered to life in the air between them. John recognized the gaunt, cruelly leering man after only a moment's reflection. It was Makka Khavazh.

"My employer sends his regrets that he could not be here personally, but he thought it courteous that you should know who had bested you. He's old-fashioned that way," the man said, conversationally, around a mouthful of chocolate.

Khavazh was an international terrorist. John remembered the file on the man. But why would he be after John? John inquired as much, and was greeted with a sardonic chuckle from his captor.

The chuckling made John ill. His enemies shared a conspiratorial look. What could all this be about? John thought of kicking the man with the holo-gauntlet in the groin with his Doc Marten steel tips if he got close enough but then he glanced down and noticed that his legs were tied to the chair.

Ideas trickled through John's brain. It was a slow

trickle, given the pounding that he had just taken. Still, he had a creeping sense that he *did* know what this was all about. Some memories just wouldn't go away.

***

"Would you like a bite?" the dark man asked, holding out the chocolate bar. John wanted to take a bite out of something else. This bastard's nose, for example. Here he was, thousands of miles away from Philadelphia, just trying to start a new relationship. Then it hit him. He was *not* just here to visit an old lab friend, or to pursue an interesting line of research. He was trying to find out if they could be more. Why had it taken him so long to piece that together? The realization --and, more to the point, the absurd timing of it-- made him laugh, despite himself.

"You think this is funny, Doctor Rutledge?" The man's abruptly menacing voice pulled John back to the moment. He knew that if he said the wrong thing, the ginger would be on him in what would surely be his last heartbeat.

Somberly, John shook his head. There was something familiar about the man's face. He was sure he'd seen it before. Finally he got a pattern-lock. It was the lack of an Indian accent that had thrown him. "'*Be happy*,'" John muttered, morosely.

"You should have taken that advice."

"I thought I did," John sighed. Deep inside, he now seethed. He realized this man traveled in disguise on the plane: sent by a terrorist to follow him. But why? He should have caught that the markings were wrong. He wore the markings of a warrior but spoke with at least the affectation of the insight of a priest. Worse still, the man fed him that cheap New Age watered-down Hindu crap that was popular at the turn on the last century. He felt like kicking himself, but, of course, his legs were still tied.

Then, belatedly, as the last of his mental defenses crumbled, John's mind became flooded with worry: What had happened to Kathryn? Where was she?

The man's face appeared a weird sort of ashen gray, as if coated with clay, making his sharp features seem etched in rock. Acid bubbled to the back of John's throat and he felt like he might vomit.

Their eyes met and then John dropped his gaze to the floor. "Where. Is. Kathryn?" he grated through clenched teeth.

"Awww," the ginger jeered in a sickly-sweet voice, "He's looking for his *girlfriend*."

"She's not my..." John started to say, just as another goon brought Kathryn in and shoved her roughly to the floor at John's feet. The man with the chocolate bar shot him a disdainful stare, and shut down the holo-projector. John felt absurdly embarrassed for denying Kathryn where she could hear. They exchange nervous glances.

"Who the freak *are* these people, John?" Kathryn demanded, defensively. "Certainly, not anyone I know."

"If I told you, would you panic?" Rutledge whispered.

"Yeah, maybe," Kathryn admitted.

"Why have you gone to such lengths to detain me? Whatever. You don't need her," he attempted to challenge, but succeeded only in entreating.

"*Why* have you gone to such *lengths* to *detain* me?" The ginger mimicked, bitterly. If looks could kill, John's stare would have iced the woman on the spot.

"Relax, Dr. Rutledge," the man insisted. "All we

want from you is some information on the GEB." The man paused for a second and then added, "and of course, a tooth."

Bewildered, John repeated, "A tooth?" Out of the corner of his eye, John saw the ginger step close.

"Come, John," the man said, walking up to Rutledge and placing his hand on his shoulder. "Don't play coy. You know the reason."

"I have no…" John started. A whirlwind of punches pummeled his face, delivered with lightning speed and merciless glee by the Ginger, interrupting his words. Simultaneously, Kathryn screamed *"STOP* it!" And rose plaintively to her knees, then tentatively, passively to her feet. He grew dizzy and his vision started to go dark, as the woman jammed a pair of needle-nosed pliers into his mouth and savagely yanked out one of his molars in a spray of blood and pain.

"Got the stem cells," the woman crowed triumphantly. The male's face brightened slightly. He started to speak.

At that moment, Kathryn slammed her right shoulder into the man who had brought her into the room, spinning so that her back then collided with his chest. She reached across to grab his gun arm in her left hand. His plasma gun discharged straight up, its searing orange blast striking the ceiling, causing smoking chunks of wood and sheet rock to fall, sizzling under the rainwater that now leaked into the room. Her right elbow connected squarely with his ribs, rewarded with a dull crack and spinning him back away from her. With her left hand she took firm control of the man's wrist and twisted it in an unnatural direction, as her right hand rose to relieve him of his weapon. She pivoted on the ball of her foot and continued the smooth motion to bend his arm

146

down and behind him, and to guide him unceremoniously to the beige-carpeted floor. John gaped in amazement, as the whole melee had taken less than two seconds.

The ginger rushed her, roaring murderously, heedless of the smoldering chunks of ceiling that rained down on her. Kathryn fired a single plasma blast, center-mass at the man on the ground. It struck him in the chest at point blank range, vaporizing much of his torso. With the same motion, Kathryn spun fluidly to bring the blaster to bear on the vicious woman with death in her eyes.

As she fired, the ginger managed to twist her body and bat the plasma rifle slightly to the right. The shot went wide and struck the wall, setting it ablaze. Flames quickly bounded up the obviously-untreated paneling. The carpet smoldered, scorched, then erupted into orange flame and heavy, acrid black smoke, which filled the room, causing John's eyes to tear up, his throat to burn. He choked. He blinked furiously to clear his eyes as he watched his not-girlfriend Kathryn battle the female assassin.

The woman struck a spin kick to Kathryn's face, sending her flying backward, knocking the blaster from her hand. It landed on the floor next to the remains of its previous owner. "Natalia!" yelled the clay-faced man, "Anatoly's here. Let's go!" Through the smoke, the assailant stalked toward her male counterpart. As an afterthought, she spun back to face a still-dazed Kathryn.

Laughing, the killer reached into her pocket, drawing her proton laser. John knew that Kathryn was defenseless. One shot and she'd be dead as nails. John struggled, wiggling his body, ripping the skin of his wrists, and managed to get the chair to fall to the side. It shattered, freeing his tied hands. Natalia pivoted and fired at him. The proton beam hit the fragments of the chair and the wood exploded into super-heated splinters. It struck dangerously close. John held tight to the wall, cursing himself for being the cause of all this.

In a desperate play, Kathyrn grabbed a gleaming chrome fire extinguisher from the wall beside her, pulled the pin, and turned the jet on Natalia as she whirled back. The flames reflected eerily off of the silvery cylinder's surface as gouts of cold white carbon dioxide gas blinded her attacker and froze the woman's face. Still Natalia fired.

Reflexively, Kathryn crouched and swept the extinguisher diagonally up over her head, in a move like an Aikido Jo staff Kata. As she raised it, the laser beam struck its mirrored surface at an oblique angle and reflected off to hit the far wall. Kathryn's body jolted back, as a needle of vapor erupted from the side of the ruptured extinguisher, but to John's surprise, she kept her footing, shifted her legs, and managed to bring the venting cylinder down on Natalia's face.

Blood spurted from the woman's shattered nose. Though coughing violently from the smoke which roiled through the room, Kathryn went Full Berserker. She pounced onto the ginger, knocking her to the floor, and smashed the extinguisher repeatedly into her increasingly-unrecognizable face.

Seeing that Kathryn was doing a fine job of bludgeoning her misbegotten assailant to a well-deserved death, John's gaze shot toward the open door. Heavy rains fell outside. Across the lot, he saw the passenger side door slide open on a rare civilian hover quad that had just touched down. Using Natalia's messy death as cover, Mr. 'Be Happy' sprinted toward the waiting craft.

Oh, *Hell* no!

The moment the man boarded and the door swung to, the quad's engines roared and the vehicle lifted itself from the muddy ground. Excited by the newfangled quad, several people approached it from behind. Bright blue plasma bolts struck out from the hover's cabin, hitting a large white propane tank, which exploded in a blinding blue-orange fireball near the gathering onlookers. The detonation sent people flying through the air.

Sheets of water roared from the heavens. The quad lifted slowly in the heavy rain, but it was gathering speed as it climbed. Ducking back into the room's inferno, John scooped the blaster from the floor next the dead goon's body. John hated killing, but he knew he had only one chance to keep the bastard from getting away. With an anguished but resolute face, he strode from the room, ignoring the drenching downpour, and the squishing of blood in his shoe from his re-opened wound. He raised the heavy blaster with both hands and fired at the rising hover quad.

The crackling orange bolt struck the quad's starboard front engine pod, causing it to explode in a hail of fire, fragments, and fan blades. Out of control, the ship rolled to the right. It clipped the top off of a tall palm tree, launching deadly coconut projectiles for many blocks around, and tumbled out of control. The wreckage corkscrewed sharply upward, then accelerated down toward the mostly-deserted city streets. John just caught a glimpse of an unsecured figure splayed against the windshield of the stricken vehicle, before it caromed into the pavement and was instantly obliterated. The deafening, concussive detonation could be heard reverberating from the nearby buildings and far-off mountains, even through the roar of the tempest. A dizzying apocalyptic flash of golden light left ghostly after-images of the neighborhood on John's retinas. Plumes of black smoke belched toward the lightning-laced black sky.

Smoke and flame and noise completely engulfed the room as John stumbled back inside. Choking from the conflagration, Kathryn still emitted low, bestial noises while slamming the fire extinguisher into the wet misshapen patch that had once been Natalia's head. John grabbed her shoulder and she spun as if to strike him with the extinguisher, primordial, feral fury in her eyes. He managed to catch it, though it was slippery with gore. Immediately, Kathryn's expression melted into a grimace of rage and tears. He reached down to lift her up, hurriedly, for the roof was beginning to give way. A wooden beam emitted a fusillade of deep, ominous snaps and cracks. John knew in seconds it would fall and crush both of them to death, then incinerate their bodies.

Unsure of the sources of his strength, John hoisted her up and half-carried her toward the door. The two darted out of the cabin, just as its ceiling collapsed in a swirling spray of angry embers that pursued them, dying, into the rain.

Lightning flashed, and thunder cracked overhead. "Where the hell are we?" John shouted above the din, his speech blurry due to the ugly swelling and mouthful of blood from Natalia's savage dentistry.

Kathryn's eyes darted around. A second later, she replied, "Other side of town."

Sirens wailed behind them. The police and fire-rescue were arriving. Impressive response time, considering. A wave of anxiety stirred up again for John. He knew he needed to call his friends at Earth Corps to help him get out of this mess. His mind cast about in panic as he realized his Earth Corps ID was back at

Kathryn's place. Then he looked at her and knew it didn't matter.

"Well, never let it be said that I'm a boring date," he cried, just managing to keep most of the hysteria out of his voice.

"No argument there!" she replied. He moved in to kiss her but she put up her hand and blocked him. "Wow, Mister! You've got a *lot* of 'splaining to do. Like why stem cells? Why *your* stem cells? And what did he mean that 'you know?' What the ***HELL***, John??"

Guns drawn, the police advanced toward them. "I promise to tell you after this. For now, say nothing." John raised his hands in the air.

"Easy to do because I know nothing," Kathryn replied. She raised her hands. The police ordered them, in harsh Spanish, to lie face down on the muddy ground. They offered no resistance when two officers came over and cuffed them.

***

Eventually the rain stopped, and a bright rainbow formed on a canvas of black clouds and dark velvety-green mountains, as the golden Tropical sun cleared the sea.

John and Kathryn had spent the last eight hours explaining the night's Mayhem to the police: Psychotic, obviously well-funded and well-connected Scary People had mistaken them for individuals of whom neither of them had ever heard. It was a lucky happenstance that they were able to escape with their lives and to neutralize some very dangerous sorts. And where, by the way, was local law enforcement while this Nightmare unfolded? John actually felt authentically offended that such a well-crafted story was gaining so little traction with these pigs. *Philistines.* With his one call, John contacted General Finney at Earth Corps. An hour later, they were both released, with abject apologies and no further questions asked.

It's who you know, John thought, sardonically, as the sun fell on his upturned face.

***

John and Kathryn made it back to her place in record time, owing to the Police escort that was offered as they left. Following a quick shower and a badly-needed change of clothes, they took a quiet booth at a yellow halogen lit café where the staff knew her name, and both ordered mocha lattes. John's Mohawk was suitably re-spiked, his razor blade safely nestled in his cheek.

Kathryn daubed foam from her lips, leaned across the table, and looked John straight in his eyes. "Now, Mister, spill. I do believe going from a Date Montage to a *crazy*-overblown Action Movie qualifies me for the Full Disclosure Package. Dig? None of this artful dodging or Emo evasion crap. I have *earned* the truth. Not least of which because I, y'know, saved your tied-to-a-chair *ass*." This was her No Bullshit Face, good as Wonder Woman's lasso, as far as John was concerned.

He sighed, and briefly studied the spiral galaxy of cinnamon floating on his untouched mocha's withering foam.

"They called it the 'Mercury Project,'" he began, at length. "My dad called it that because it was supposed to be man's message to the gods: 'We are rising.' Soon, we would be like them. I mean, Hubris much?"

"Thought you were just a lab technician," she

152

lilted almost sternly, through glossy black lipstick.

"I was. My dad ran the project. For an eleven-year-old, I had a massive amount of input."

Lustrous blue and pink highlights from the neon sign over the espresso machine danced over her incredulous face. "Eleven?"

"'Massively gifted.' 140 IQ. I was considered a genius. Especially with genetics."

Their eyes locked. "You still are, John," she breathed. But The 'Last Biopunk' brushed off the comment. He'd trained his mind to recoil from any invitation for his narcissism. And genius cut both ways, as he knew only too well.

Sucking in a deep breath, he knew that it was now or never. Either he shared it and she left screaming or...Well he really did not venture to guess what the other outcome could be. Exhaling, he found his voice. "The six-thousand-gene sequence that forms the basis for the GEBs' intelligence is --um-- mine."

"What?"

"My dad…" John reflexively bit back. "No, you're right. It *is* time for the truth. I've told myself the lie so many times I *almost* completely believe it. Even used the anger to hold my dad off at arm's length so *he* wouldn't have to focus on it." John stopped and wiped a surprising tear from his eye. He sucked in a deep breath. "I told my dad my DNA should be used in the project. He opposed it at first. There was a ton of controversy at the time. Leftists were attacking our lab, believing --rightly, as it turns out-- that the only people who could afford the procedure were the wealthy. It would be the ultimate and final barrier of inequity. On the other side, the far-right religious groups felt we were playing God."

"By Jove, where would they ever get *that* idea?"

John let out a sad, pathetic laugh. "My DNA was not scheduled, but being a very industrious Tween, I switched the sample one night, made some tweaks. I was just playing around, showing off. Wasn't supposed to be found. But I forgot to turn off the damn terminal, so there it all was, sitting in active memory, when the lab opened the next day. We...When my father found out, he was furious. He made me swear never to tell anyone. My dad told me every day, multiple times that he was sorry for 'switching the sample.' It was weird how his change of the story just slowly muscled out the truth. When the mental and emotional side effects started to show up in the GEB, I forced myself to believe what he said. The reward was not having to face problems like this."

"Stockholm Syndrome," she said, softly.

John shrugged, not sure if she was serious or joking. Finally, he continued. "More like 'Double-think.' Anyway, I was so angry at him for so long, and all he was trying to do was protect me."

Looking at her face, John could tell that the story was a lot for her to take in. Several awkward moments passed before she replied. "You'll make it right, John," she said softly, warmth and sympathy in her eyes. "I know you will," and then she changed the subject. John felt his heart lift and fall.

Kathryn asked him what was happening back in the US. He became quiet. His eyes searched the room and fixated on the music from the cafe's speakers. It was an old jazz tune that he hadn't heard in years. *Someone to Watch Over Me*, he believed it was. He finally took a sip of his lukewarm Mocha, wiped his mouth with the back of his hand, and began to explain about what happened after the GEB wars. Kathryn's contact lenses grew a darker, more melancholy blue the more he talked about the GEB wars. After a while, John decided to stop, knowing that if he kept talking, he would just cause her more pain.

"Kathryn, I… I'm sorry if that triggered the memories," He started.

"No. Look, it's fine. Just thought that..." Kathryn stopped abruptly. Her mouth pressed against folded hands, her elbows resting dejectedly on the dark wooden tabletop. "I wish you weren't going. Stay here. With me."

"I wish I could stay. *Gods* do I wish I could! But I have to get back to my lab and the work. Why not come back with *me*?"

"You know I can't. They killed my father and left my mother to die in jail."

"My point," John breathed, ruefully. "I really want this to work," John cried out, quietly, the uncharacteristically artless squeak in his voice a sign of utter sincerity. The moment stretched, and John finally took a deep, composure-restoring breath.

"So," he began, his voice growing steadier, "I was thinking about your research."

"Was this *before* or *after* we were fighting psychopathic assassins in a burning building, and shooting down enemy aircraft?"

"Listen, you! It was...well actually *during*, some of it," he confessed.

"I'll remember that during the months of therapy I'm looking at right now."

"Send me the bill for that, willya? So, speaking of remembering..."

John launched into a lengthy exposition on the strengths and weaknesses of her research design. It was not enough just to remove the memories. Nature abhors a vacuum, and lacking data, the mind would likely regress into delusion to account for the missing times. A replacement memory set would need to be imprinted. He quickly sketched a design for her, laying out the basic mechanism, literally on the back of a napkin. He handed it to her and she snapped a picture of it with her comm, then tore up the napkin and dropped the pieces into her large mug to soak away in the last of her mocha. "This should be enough to get you started," he offered.

Kathryn's contacts leapt from somber to ebullient blue, even as her eyes still held the sign of sadness. Not for the first time, John wondered why she wore the lenses, Kathryn was not the sort to hide her emotions; as the old saying went, she wore her heart on her sleeve.

Still, they added another channel by which he could watch her lighting up. And that made him happy.

Oh god how I want this to work! His mind screamed.

But John realized, wearily, that there were a great many memories yet to make before that could ever come to pass.

WWW.JELLINGTONASHTON.COM

Thank you for reading Mechanical Error. Please consider leaving a review to share your thoughts and opinions. While you're there, tell us about your favorite classic creature feature film.

90367330R00093

Made in the USA
Middletown, DE
22 September 2018